REUNION

WRAK-ASHWEA: THE AGE OF LIGHT
BOOK ONE

LEIGH ROBERTS

DRAGON WINGS PRESS

CONTENTS

Dedication v

Chapter 1 1
Chapter 2 7
Chapter 3 25
Chapter 4 57
Chapter 5 79
Chapter 6 91
Chapter 7 103
Chapter 8 117
Chapter 9 141
Chapter 10 155
Chapter 11 173
Chapter 12 195
Chapter 13 201
Chapter 14 215
Chapter 15 231
Chapter 16 251
Chapter 17 265

Interviews 277
Please Read 281
Acknowledgments 283

ISBN: 978-1-951528-38-6 (ebook)
ISBN: 978-1-951528-39-3 (paperback)

Dedication

To those of you whose hearts yearn for the answer to—

What If?

CHAPTER 1

Pan turned to Moart'Tor as they watched the last day of the High Council assembly. They were unseen by the others as Pan's powers allowed them to be present yet undetectable. "Tell me, Moart'Tor, what you have learned by being here?"

Pan waited while Moart'Tor collected his thoughts. He finally looked up, and Pan saw the deep compassion and sadness in his eyes.

"They are just like us. They love. They care for their offling, they protect them, and they provide for them. They laugh together and praise the Great Spirit."

"So answer me one last question. Where is the abomination?"

Moart'Tor lowered his head. "The only abomination I know of is the hatred in my father's heart."

Pan reached out and touched the side of his face gently so he would look up.

"Look at me, Moart'Tor, son of Dak'Tor, son of Moc'Tor and E'ranale, kin to Straf'Tor from the time of the Fathers-of-Us-All. I need your help. Not only to save the Akassa and Sassen, but if there is any way, also to save those at Zuenerth."

"Will you stand with me?"

Moart'Tor fell to his knees and covered his face with his hands. "Yes, Guardian. I will stand with you. Tell me what you want me to do."

"You cannot go back to Zuenerth. There would be too many questions, and they would know you are withholding something, and the Sassen living with you at Kayerm need to return to their own lives."

Pan then leaned down and placed her hand on top of Moart'Tor's bowed head. "Rise, then. There is much for you to learn."

Thousands of miles away, in a place of antiquity, Wrollonan'Tor turned to his daughter, Irisa. "Prepare a place for them at Lulnomia. Pan is returning home, and she is bringing Moart'Tor with her."

Acaraho would have been glad to be home had Adia returned with him. Though he knew why she had stayed at the Far High Hills, he missed her at his side. He missed casually sharing the day's events as they enjoyed the pleasure of being cuddled up together,

her head resting on his shoulder and one leg thrown over his midsection. The scent of pine in her hair. Her warm breath on his skin. How small and delicate her hand felt as her fingers intertwined with his.

He also missed Nootau. It would be good to have him and his mate, Iella, here with them. He wondered how long it might be before the situation with Moart'Tor would be resolved and they could all travel to the High Rocks.

After the High Council meeting, when Chief Kotori and Tiponi had returned to their village, the Chief called Awantia to his shelter. She ducked down to enter and saw both waiting for her. The Chief motioned for her to sit, and she lowered herself to the ground, arranging her skirts to sit cross-legged. She stretched her hands out to warm them at the fire in the center of the shelter while the smoke exited through the hole above made specifically for this purpose.

"After much thought, Tiponi and I have decided it is you who will accompany the Waschini, Ned Webb, when the time comes for him to travel to the other villages to teach our people Whitespeak."

Awantia wanted to ask why she had been selected but was not sure if she should. She did not want to appear to be questioning the Chief's decision.

Luckily, Tiponi seemed to read her mind. "The Chief has chosen you for many reasons. You are skilled; you are a great teacher. You are free to travel with the Waschini as you have no life-walker and children to tie you down here. Your light-hearted wit will pave the way into the hearts of those at the other Chiefs' villages, just as it has here. Everyone loves and respects you, Awantia. Do you not know that?"

Awantia shook her head. "I have never thought that of myself, not any of those things you have said. And Ned Webb, he knows nothing of this yet?"

"No. But as soon as he returns, we will tell him," Tiponi explained. "He went with Oh'Dar to Chief Is'Taqa's village to see off the other Waschini, the one called Newell Storis."

Awantia wondered if Ned Webb would indeed return. He had come to them to learn how to live their ways and then decided he missed his Waschini life and family too much to stay. What was there to say he would not do the same again? But she said none of that. After all, he would either return or not.

"Thank you for the opportunity to serve our people. I will not fail you or them."

The Chief waved his hand to dismiss her, but just before she stepped out of the shelter, he spoke once more. "Our faith in you is not misplaced, and when the time comes for you to set out with him, know that you will be missed at our fires. Our prayers will go with you, and we will welcome your return."

Awantia couldn't wait to tell her friend, Myrica, and went directly to find her. "I know who they are sending with Ned Webb."

Myrica looked up from pounding corn into flour. "Tell me what you have heard, and please say it is not me."

"It is not anything I have heard. Chief Kotori and Tiponi told me themselves, just now."

"Why would the Chief tell you unless— Is it you?" Myrica stopped her work.

"Yes. I am humbled by their faith in me."

"They could not have chosen better. I am happy for you—if you are happy?"

"Yes, I am."

"Your face does not agree."

"I am. Truly. I am feeling the weight of it, that is all."

"Everyone will be happy to hear this; you will see. Oh! Were you hoping it would be me? Hoping that if I spent enough time with him, I would fall in love? Please tell me that is not why you look uncertain about being selected?"

Awantia couldn't tell her friend her uncertainty was nothing to do with that. It was because she feared that she herself had fallen in love with Ned Webb.

CHAPTER 2

Newell Storis was on his way to Wilde Edge, and Oh'Dar and Ned were back at Kthama. Oh'Dar was anxious to spend time with his life-walker, Acise, and their daughter, I'Layah, but first had to get Ned connected with others there. He introduced Ned to Mapiya, the females' representative, and High Protector Awan, both of whom would help as needed.

"Where do I start?" Ned asked Oh'Dar as they were following Mapiya to Ned's living quarters.

"Chief Kotori will select someone to travel with you to the different villages, but before that, you must learn how to teach. That is where my grandmother can help. She has been teaching our people Whitespeak for some time, and she can explain the methods that have been most successful."

"So others here speak English?"

"You will be surprised how many."

"That is a great comfort, Grayson. I will have many benefits living here that you did not."

"Language wasn't a disadvantage. I learned Handspeak first, like all the offspring. It makes sense; children have basic motor control before they can form words. Then I learned English and the language of the People and the Brothers in the same way you learned English. When Haan and his people appeared, that was a more difficult one. But we managed it by using Handspeak in combination with speech, to compensate for their accent, which is stronger due to their mouth structure and those large canines."

"Yes, I've noticed the canines."

"Here we are." Oh'Dar stepped aside to let Ned pass in front of him through the woven wood door Mapiya had just opened.

"This is one of the brighter rooms, and the fluorite will recharge faster in here," Mapiya explained. "When spring returns and the angle of the sun's rays shifts, it will get even lighter,"

"It is dark at Kthama, to be sure. And cool," Ned observed, running his hands over the smooth rock walls as he walked around the perimeter of the room. "Oh!" he exclaimed.

"Walls like that serve as mirrors. They have been polished to create a reflection, blurry though it is," Oh'Dar explained.

"I suppose everyone wants to look their best," Ned said.

"It is a little more than that. Slowly, it seems more and more of the People are adopting some type of clothing, even only as decoration, so these mirrors help. That wasn't always the case. The males' attitudes have been changing slowly, influenced by our previous Leader, Khon'Tor. Then my father and brother started adopting the idea. Before, only the females and some of the elderly males wore any clothing. The males pretty much walked about naked."

"Are you serious?" Ned turned from his wavy reflection to look at Oh'Dar.

"They have so much hair that they didn't really look naked. For the most part, they looked like they were wearing hairy breechcloths, but the elderly still needed something around them."

"So interesting. I couldn't imagine walking around basically naked."

"It didn't feel like that to them," Oh'Dar chuckled.

"Everything here is unusual to me, like a dream. I hope I never awaken," Ned added.

"You have taken on a huge responsibility. To teach the Brothers English is no small feat, but it will be critical if they are to help the Waschini find their way back into harmony with the Great Spirit."

"You and I are the Waschini."

"Yes, that is true. It was sometimes hard for me to recognize who I really was at any given point. I am

Waschini. I am one of the People. I am one of the Brothers."

"I can see how that could be dizzying at times. But, gracious, Oh'Dar. Take yourself out of it and step back and think about how amazing that is. You are living a life no one else has ever lived. Your story will be told for generations and generations."

Oh'Dar thought of the story his mother had told him about her mother's dream.

"You know my mother died giving birth to me," Adia had said. "But just before I was born, she told my father about a dream she had the night before. She was in a beautiful forest, and the sky overhead was a deep blue. So deep a blue that it was unnatural, and it struck her so. As she was standing there, dark clouds formed, and the wind picked up.

Before long, the weather became so strong that she was frightened. The darker the skies became, the more her fear grew. She found a small alcove to hide in, and just as she thought the storm would overtake her, the skies cleared, and a bird with the brightest blue feathers she had ever seen landed before her.

He carried a beautiful stone in his beak and laid it at her feet. As she bent to pick it up, the bird spoke. He said he was sent by the Great Spirit to tell her that the daughter she was carrying would become a great blessing to the People. And that through this daughter would come another great blessing, and she would name him Oh'Dar. Then the bird flew away, and my mother woke up with a great feeling of peace and calm. The next morning, she died, giving me life."

He nodded. "Let's hope we are successful and that there will be generations and generations to pass that story on."

Oh'Dar, Acise, and Ned sat with Acaraho, Awan, Mapiya, Ben, and Miss Vivian. Nadiwani was absent, taking care of I'Layah so Acise and Oh'Dar could have some time together. As they were eating, Haan approached.

Acaraho motioned for him to join them, but the Sassen Leader shook his head. "I have come with word from Chief Kotori. He has decided who will accompany Ned to the other villages when the time comes. Also, Pan and Moart'Tor have left. My people will be returning home from Kayerm over the next day or so."

"Left? To where?" Acaraho asked.

"That information was not made available to me. Only that he will be safely far away from Kthama."

It was then that Acaraho realized Haan and Pan had not spoken together and that this was one of the instances in which knowledge was given to the Sassen Leader as if from nowhere. Just as it sometimes was to Nootau.

"Safely? Did he make threats against our people —yours or mine?" Acaraho asked.

"No, just meaning that your mate and offspring can return home as there is no longer any danger that Moart'Tor will be able to sense the existence of the An'Kru, the Promised One."

Acaraho let out a long deep sigh, and the tension left his jaw and shoulders.

"I will send word to the Far High Hills," High Protector Awan offered.

"And I will have the Leader's Quarters and offspring's sleeping areas freshened up," Mapiya said brightly. "Soon, you will be reunited, and things will return to normal!"

"Thank you both," Acaraho said. "Now is a time of preparation. Though we do not know what is coming, we know at least what our parts are. The Brothers must learn Whitespeak. The Waschini might not be able to return to our territory, thanks to you, Oh'Dar, but that does not mean they will not go after those located elsewhere."

Oh'Dar knew, despite the positive words, that Acaraho feared things would never return to normal —at least not for a long time. He felt a pang of anxiety; he had so wanted some quiet time with his family, to live a normal life, but the harder he tried, the further it seemed to slip out of reach. Newell's words rang through his head. He had to see the Governor. He had to bring the power of the Morgan name to bear, in whatever ways he could, to stave off the persecution of the Brothers.

Acise reached over and squeezed Oh'Dar's hand.

He knew she had seen his reaction. How long could they bear up under this?

"I am sorry, son," Ben said, glancing over at him. "I know the last thing you want to do is leave again. You just got home."

"I am exhausted. And angry. And ashamed. All at once. I will do what I can, but I fear it will not be enough. If the Waschini are hell-bent on stealing the Brothers' land, it will take more than the Morgan name to change their minds."

"How strange," Acise said, "that someone can steal something that is no one's to own. Our people do not own the land. We are good stewards of the rich resources that are freely given for our benefit. The Waschini would take what is no man's to take from another, the blessings and provision of the Great Spirit."

Oh'Dar looked at Ben and slowly shook his head. "It is not enough for the Brothers to learn Whitespeak. Something must prepare the hearts of our people to be open to an entirely new way of thinking. We share the same planet, but we are living in separate worlds, and I fear that in the end, only one world will survive."

Haan's people settled back into their home, Kht'shWea, glad to see their friends and the rest of their families again. However, Naahb noticed that his sister, Eitel, seemed to have lost her smile. He asked her about it, though he was sure he knew the source of her sadness.

"You are not happy to be home," he said to her one morning at first meal.

"Of course I am," she replied, her voice lackluster.

"You are sad that Moart'Tor has left us; you cannot fool me," he said gently.

"Alright, yes, I am. I know you do not approve of my interest in him, though I also know it was out of your concern for my well-being."

"If you had continued down the path you were on, it would only have led to heartbreak. It was clear, despite his initial reaction, that Moart'Tor was also attracted to you. But there was a real risk you could never safely have borne his offspring. You must know I speak the truth."

Eitel sighed, "I know, it is true. My mind can reason it out, but my heart still wants to be with him, to see where it might have gone."

"It is far past time for you to be paired. I have spoken with Mother and Father, and they agree. Moart'Tor will not be back. The best thing you can do for yourself is to approach Haan and then ask Bidzel and Yuma'qia to find a match for you. We are from Notar's community; there is no reason they will not find you a safe breeding mate."

"A safe breeding mate." With a stick, she skewered a piece of hot cooked fish from the spit and blew on it. "It sounds less than enticing."

"I am told you will not feel that way once your offspring moves in your water cradle and you hold him or her in your arms for the first time," he tried to soothe his sister.

She put the piece of fish into her mouth and slowly chewed it. Then she acquiesced, "You are right, I know. I will think about it."

Adia was in the Healer's Quarters with Urilla Wuti and thrilled at the news that she could soon return home. But despite the happy tidings, the Healer knew both she and her people were standing on the precipice of far-sweeping change.

From the time she had come to Kthama to become the Healer to the People of the High Rocks, there had been a seemingly constant series of challenges. Her heart longed for the routine, the mundane. Perhaps even to have a day of being bored. What would that feel like? To have everything so predictable that one actually wanted something to happen to shake things up? She couldn't imagine that day coming—certainly not any time soon.

"I am sure Eyota will return with me to Kthama," she said to Urilla Wuti. "She came here to keep me company, and I know she misses Clah, while he no doubt misses her and their daughter, Tansy, in return."

"The problem is always that the twelve cannot be anywhere near the same place as An'Kru. Pan never fully explained what would happen, but nothing good. So if Eyota goes back with you, we are back to always being aware of their whereabouts relative to An'Kru's."

"I know," Adia sighed. "I am ready for springtime. Rebirth. Restart. I love seeing the blooms poking up from the soil as the Great Mother's promise of renewal."

She looked over at her sleeping twins, Aponi and Nelairi, in their cozy nest. It was a struggle not to think of Nootau and Nimida every time she looked at them. She seemed to be struggling to find happiness lately. Of course, part of it was that the Guardian Pan would be taking An'Kru away when he was seven years old. Where would they go? Would he be happy there? She couldn't bear the idea of his being unhappy. How long would he be gone? How old would he be, and what would he be like when he returned? Offspring were supposed to bring joy, but she struggled with the challenges that, for her, seemed always to come with motherhood.

Iella entered, and Adia and Urila Wuti both looked up at her, warm smiles on their faces. Urilla

Wuti stretched out her hand, beckoning Iella to sit next to them.

"Apricoria is settling in, but she misses her parents," said Iella. "And she misses the Deep Valley. This is much more like the High Rocks, is it not Adia?"

"Yes. The High Rocks and the Far High Hills are very similar in their mountainous surroundings and the size of the cave systems."

Iella sat down on the floor next to the other two females. "Is it true that a path from Kht'shWea up to the Guardians' meadow blooms earlier than anywhere else, and the most profusely?"

"Yes, it does. Not only the path flourishes with life, but the entire meadow it leads to. Deer, foxes, and birds all linger there because of the peace and the bounty. The fruit trees and berry bushes bear earlier and produce much larger fruits, and the twelve generator stones are an amazing sight. They are beautiful anytime, but when the sun's rays hit their surfaces, they sparkle and glimmer, almost as if they were alive. You can feel the life force of the Great Mother there, Iella, more than in any other place. You will see for yourself."

"Are we allowed to go there?" Iella's eyebrows rose.

"With reverence, yes. From what I know, the Sassen Guardians do not assemble there often. I heard Pan say that most of their teaching is taking place in the Corridor."

"I have never been to the Corridor," Iella said wistfully. "There is so much I have to learn."

"Oh, little niece." Urilla Wuti leaned over and touched Iella's arm. "You know so much more than you realize. But yes, there are wonders awaiting you, that is for sure. Now tell us about Apricoria."

"The vision she was given of the future has disturbed her deeply. Harak'Sar put her in a room near mine and Nootau's, and I think that helped. I am trying to keep her busy. Of course, taking care of Chief Kotori's village took up a lot of time, and I think it was good for her to be so involved in something so important right away. It is harder to keep sad feelings away when the days are so routine."

"I was just longing for routine," said Adia. "But now that you have said that—"

Urilla Wuti looked over at her friend. "I wish I could break this cloud which is hanging over you, Adia. It is not like you to be so depressed."

Nootau came up behind his mate, who was working at the food counter in their quarters. He put his arms around her waist and pulled her closer. Her quiet moan of pleasure brought a smile to his face. "How do you feel about going to Kthama?"

She leaned back against him, letting her head fall onto his strong shoulder. He was built so much like his father, Acaraho, and his physical height and strength were a comfort to her in so many ways.

"I will miss my parents, of course. But our homes are not that far apart. Though, if we had offspring, I know my mother would hate us being away."

Nootau buried his nose in her hair, "Hopefully, that will happen sometime soon. Though I know what you are saying about your parents." He continued to nuzzle her ear, and he heard a clink as she set the cutting tools down on the rock table. He turned her to face him, and they shared a deep, lingering kiss.

Then he brushed the hair from her face, leaned down, caught her behind her knees, and swept her up into his arms. He gently carried her over to the sleeping mat, where they shared a quiet afternoon of lovemating.

When they were finished, Iella said, "I am always amazed at how things work out. Here we are going to Kthama, where you will be able to spend time not only with An'Kru but also with your new brother and sister."

Nootau propped himself up on his elbow so he could see his mate's soulful eyes. He toyed with a strand of her hair. "And how perfect that Apricoria will be here to apprentice with Urilla Wuti while you apprentice to my mother."

"I am looking forward to that; there is always something new to learn, and I so enjoy Adia's company. Both your parents are such wonderful souls, Nootau. You have been doubly blessed."

Nootau lay down again. He wanted so much to tell Iella about Nimida being his sister. He needed her counsel and support. He had not known the truth that long himself, but the longer he waited, the more disingenuous he felt about not telling his mate. Did he need to ask his mother's permission? It was her story to tell, not his. But it was also his story. He was confused, and he had learned that when in confusion was not the time to act. It would come to him, at the right time and in the right way, and he would wait for that guidance, though he prayed it would not be long in coming.

He realized he was feeling sorry for himself, and instead, he thought of his mother's journey. Taken Without Consent and then having to bear the social judgment year after year for a sin she did not commit. Next, having to choose which of her offspring to give up to Khon'Tor's spiteful and evil mate. And Acaraho, willingly stepping in and bearing the shame—shame that was neither of theirs to bear. No doubt seeing the sideways glances, the conversations that stopped when one of them walked by. His mother had told him that, in time, the People had accepted her and Acaraho and forgiven them, but he knew things could still sometimes be awkward.

What of Khon'Tor? What did Khon'Tor feel? Nootau knew for himself the miraculous change that had come over Khon'Tor, now no longer the male who assaulted his mother. And it was affirmed with every action the former Leader took. How he loved his mate, Tehya, and their offspring.

And Nootau had two fathers. Acaraho, who had raised him despite not being of the same blood. The second, whose blood he did carry, he could never publicly acknowledge.

A shudder ran through him as he contemplated how trapped his mother must have felt.

"What is wrong? Are you cold?" Iella reached down and pulled the hide covering up.

"Oh, no, just lost in thought. The People of the High Rocks will love you, but not as much as I do."

"Will you return with us to Kthama?" Adia asked Eyota as they were sitting together in their favorite place on the bank of the shallows at the Far High Hills. It was a setting similar to Kthama and helped them feel less homesick

"Yes. I miss Clah, and he has not had any time with our daughter. And besides, I would miss you, Adia." She reached out and lightly patted her friend's smaller hand.

Adia readjusted An'Kru's position. "I am glad you are coming home with us. I would miss you too." She smiled.

"I am a little jealous, though," Eyota said. "I did

not get to see this Moart'Tor. The only Mothoc we have seen is Pan. It would be fascinating to see another of the Ancients. You said he had coloring much like Pan's?"

"That is how it was described to me. I did not get to see him, either. Where has Pan taken him? Do you not wonder?"

"Yes, I do. Sometimes it is all I can think about. Where has Pan been living these thousands of years? Is she alone? Does she have friends? Or does she leave her body somewhere safe and inhabit the Corridor? Her mother would be there, and her father."

What Eyota said made perfect sense. Having seen her father in the Corridor, Adia could easily have stayed there with him, back safe in his embrace. She had wondered many times if perhaps that was why the Corridor was not commonly made known to them. If people knew how wonderful the next life was, would they not rush to end their lives on Etera? Life was difficult, at best, yet in the Corridor, there was such beauty, peace, and unity.

"You have been there," Eyota said.

"Yes, several times. I met Pan's mother, E'ranale, and once, my father."

Eyota's mouth fell open. "Oh please, can you tell me about it?"

"It was as if every longing I ever had was fulfilled. All the dreams of seeing loved ones again, and then there you are, with them. Just as real as us here together, only deeper and more present. There are no words to describe the joy of that reunion—and in a place of such beauty. The experiences in the Corridor make this life seem like a shadow cast by what we know."

"Where was it? Where were you?"

"I was here, on Etera, actually. Only it was more — Enriched is maybe the word. I was in a beautiful meadow, with birdsong, only more melodic and sweeter than you could imagine. And the trees bloomed with the deepest and brightest flowers ever. Kthama's mountain range was on the horizon, with a beautiful blueish mist falling down over the peaks. Every single element was enchanting. Even the grass under my feet felt more alive—as if it was reaching up to cradle and welcome my feet. I have never felt such complete acceptance and love."

"You saw your father there. Did you ever see your mother?"

Adia looked down to the side. "No. I never got to see my mother, and I have often wondered why; surely she is there somewhere. But time is different there. I will not even try to explain it. When E'ranale explained it to me, it seemed as if I almost understood it, but whatever little bit I did grasp is gone now."

"But the Corridor is not where we go when we die?"

"No. It is only one step on the way to our return to the Great Spirit, so if that was not reunion with the

Great Spirit, if that was not going Home, then my mind cannot grasp what it will be like. I cannot imagine anything more blissful than what I experienced there."

Just then, Tansy let out a loud burp, and both of them laughed.

"Well, that brought us back to reality," Eyota remarked, bringing her daughter up over her shoulder and gently patting her back.

Tansy turned her head, and Adia found herself staring into the offspring's beautiful grey eyes. The same grey eyes as her son. An'Kru, the Promised One. What future awaited him? In her heart of hearts, Adia was not sure she wanted to know.

CHAPTER 3

Moart'Tor looked up in the direction Pan was pointing. Somehow, they were no longer at Kayerm. In the wink of an eye, a massive mountain range lay stretched out in front of them, tall snow-capped peaks glistening in the sun. Heavy layers of snow carpeted the lower reaches, and there was a thick dusting on the fir trees that covered the mountainside beyond. It was breathtakingly beautiful and delightfully cool. The air was crisp and sharp and felt somehow cleansing.

"Where are we, Guardian?" he finally asked, tearing his gaze away from the beauty that lay before him.

"This is Lulnomia. Home to the remaining Ancients and their sons and daughters. Home to the Mothoc who still serve Etera and all her creatures."

"There— This— There are others here?" Moart'Tor felt a mixture of emotions arising within him. An ache of homesickness for a life of companionship and unity he had never known. Sudden anxiety as he wondered if the other Mothoc would accept him when they knew he was one of the rebels. Relief that there truly were other Ancients still alive and living in community.

"Yes. This is where all the Mothoc from every community came after we left the Akassa and the Sassen. I will explain it to you in time. It was one of the most difficult decisions I ever had to make. Not the most difficult one, however. No, that one came later."

"Oh, if my father only knew of this place. If the others did. This might be enough to sway them from their quest to destroy them."

"Perhaps. Though from what you have said of him, I am not sure even the blessings of Lulnomia are enough to quell your father's hatred. Come, we will walk the rest of the way."

While Moart'Tor's heart was pounding in anticipation, with each step across the snowy landscape, Pan's was breaking. Rohm'Mok, her beloved, and their daughter, Tala—what had become of them? When she left, she had beseeched Rohm'Mok to find another. Someone to be a mate to him and mother to Tala, but now that request haunted her.

Pan's sister, Vel, was to lead those who had come from the High Rocks. And what of Hatos'Mok, who had tried to exile Pan? Had he continued as Overseer? Pan had lived with Wrollonan'Tor for thousands of years, and in all that time, never asked about Lulnomia, never wanted to know what had happened after she left. She had remanded it to the Order of Functions because her path had required her elsewhere, and to look back would only have made harder what was hers to do.

And yet here she was. In a few moments, the questions she had not let herself ask would be answered. Whether she was ready or not.

Up the long path she walked, one foot in front of the other. Did they know she was coming? Would they be waiting for her? Wrollonan'Tor and his daughter, Irisa, would be aware she was returning but had they told any of the other Mothoc?

No matter. She would know soon enough.

Finally, they reached the Great Entrance. Thousands of years ago, Pan had taken her last steps through Lulnomia, leaving the empty halls behind her. She had asked for that. To be able to leave in private. It was hard enough as it was, and she did not want other eyes to witness her heartbreak. Now she felt the same. So many memories, so many emotions were being stirred within her.

The Guardian stepped inside Lulnomia. It took all her strength, but it was what she had to do. And she had never shirked what was hers to do.

She took in the white stone floors, the high ceiling made of frozen rock and ice with the iridescent beauty of the snow crystals sparkling in the daylight that broke through the entrance behind her.

She had lost all thought of Moart'Tor. Once again, she was back where she'd had to say goodbye to everything that mattered to her. That had been the price; that was her sacrifice. It had cost her everything to save it all.

Out of the shadows stepped a huge figure. Pan smiled. A friend. Perhaps one of the few she had here. Wrollonan'Tor took another step forward, and Moart'Tor snapped his head around. His jaw dropped at the silver-coated behemoth standing before him.

"I am Wrollonan'Tor, Guardian of the Ancients. This is Lulnomia."

Moart'Tor looked at Pan, confusion creasing his face. "Another Guardian? I thought—"

"As you will learn, my brother's son, much of what we believed to be true has been proven otherwise."

He looked around. "Where is everyone else?"

"They are here, just a whisper away," Wrollonan'Tor said. "I wanted to greet you in private, but you will meet them in a moment. Trust me."

Wrollonan'Tor took another step toward Pan and Moart'Tor. Moart'Tor stepped backward. "You, you could destroy us all. I can feel the power radiating off you."

"I could, but so could Pan, for I have been her teacher through the thousands of years since she left this place. Her abilities now nearly rival my own."

"Have I been brought here to be killed?"

Moart'Tor looked almost frantically at Pan and then back to Wrollonan'Tor. "Is that why we are here? Is that my punishment for lying to you?"

Pan's heart reached out to him, and she placed a hand on his shoulder. "Of course not."

"You have been brought here for the chance to redeem your soul," Wrollonan'Tor said. "And to discover who you truly are, who you were meant to be. A life awaits you here, son of Dak'Tor, among the rest of the Mothoc who serve the Great Spirit."

Then he turned to Pan. "Are you ready, daughter of Moc'Tor and E'ranale?"

"I am."

In the next instant, Wrollonan'Tor was gone, but Pan and Moart'Tor were not alone. A collective gasp went up from a crowd that had seemingly instantly materialized in the Great Entrance.

At that moment, Moart'Tor realized that Wrollonan'Tor's power had concealed them from the other Mothoc, just as Pan's had while they were at the Far High Hills. But—a Mothoc who could cloak others even from his own kind? Moart'Tor had no idea that kind of power existed. And so, in truth, the others had not appeared; they had been there all along.

"Pan! The Guardian has returned!" Mothoc voices rose, and people pointed in their direction. Mothers bent down to explain to their offling, who were unprepared for such a miracle. Some people froze in place, not believing what they were seeing, while others ran to tell anyone they could find.

Within a few moments, the Great Entrance of Lulnomia was even fuller.

Pan looked over the faces staring back at her. Time had passed. As a Guardian, she had not aged, but they had. The Mothoc lived a long time, but they didn't live forever. Pan could not help but notice that the oldest of them, those elders who had left Kthama with Moc'Tor and Straf'Tor, were nearing the end of their life cycles, and the weariness of long life was showing on their faces.

She recognized a great number of everyone present, including Wosot and Kyana, with their warm smiles, which Pan only then realized how much she needed to see. A male coming to the front looked like an older Norland, the Leader of Kayerm. It had to be. And there were Oragur and Neilith. She was sure it was them. Even Toniss was there, and though she was considerably older, she was still alive, and Pan was grateful to see her familiar face. Trac was not with her, and all over again, Pan was hit by the amount of time that had passed since she left Lulnomia. She wondered if he had returned to the Great Spirit.

The crowd continued to grow as others arrived at the back, pushing forward those already there. Her eyes searched the crowd, looking for the one she longed and feared most to see. The crowd parted, and Irisa stepped up to the front.

"The Guardian Pan has come back to Lulnomia. As is her right!" Then Irisa turned and faced Pan.

"Welcome home. They have waited long for your return."

Pan's heart was breaking. Where was the face she longed to see? Though it might bring heartbreak, though he might have another at his side, she still needed to see him. *Please, oh please, Great Spirit, let Rohm'Mok still walk Etera.* Let him still live.

The crowd parted again.

A tall male slipped through the gap and stood motionless. Staring at her a moment, he said only one word. "Pan."

She could not help herself; she walked directly over to stand in front of Rohm'Mok, her beloved, and stared into his eyes, looking for the answers she needed. His eyes were locked on hers.

Before anything more could happen, another figure stepped out to the front and stood next to Rohm'Mok. Vel. Pan's sister Vel. Had she ruled Kthama all this time as Pan had decreed? The Guardian watched Vel place a hand on Rohm'Mok's shoulder. A hand of compassion, of comfort. Of familiarity.

Oh, no. Had Vel and Rohm'Mok found love together? Was it her sister who had taken Pan's place in her beloved's heart? Pan had asked for and been granted Bak'tah-Awhidi, and was that not what she had prayed for, that Rohm'Mok would find another to walk his life with and to be a mother to their daughter, Tala? Yet she had not considered it might be with her own sister.

Pan steeled herself to face the future she had made possible. She had set Rohm'Mok free and had only herself to blame that he had done just as she asked. This was not his fault or Vel's. This was her doing, and she had no right to blame them for any of it.

Pan tore her eyes away from Rohm'Mok. "Vel, my sister. My heart leaps with joy to see you again." Vel reached out and hugged Pan.

"You said you would return," Rohm'Mok said. "I did not know if I would live to see the day."

She gathered all her willpower to press back the tears that were stinging her eyes.

Pan's other sister, Inrion, stepped forward and held out her arms for Pan's embrace before turning to a female standing next to her. "Tala, this is Pan, Guardian of Etera."

Pan hadn't thought her heart could break any further after seeing Rohm'Mok next to Vel, but then it did. Tala, her daughter, now grown. All the years of her upbringing were lost to Pan. Someone else now filled her daughter's memories and mother's place.

"So, you are my mother. I am pleased to meet you." Tala held out her hand as if she wanted Pan to take it.

Pan touched her daughter's fingers—the hand that had held on to hers both for comfort and in times of happiness. It was no longer small, no longer the precious little hand that had been so protectively swallowed up by her own.

"There is much to tell and much to ask," Rohm'Mok said. "I pray there will be time for all of that."

Pan turned to Moart'Tor, who had been standing quietly stalwart through the reunion. "No doubt many of you expected I would only return to bring to you the Promised One, but that time is not at hand. This is Moart'Tor, son of Dak'Tor, son of Moc'Tor and E'ranale, and kin to Straf'Tor from the time of the Fathers-of-Us-All. He was born into the group Straf'Tor expelled from Kayerm. Yes, there is much to tell here, but now is not the time. He is of my blood, and he is a friend, and I do ask that he be welcomed into your community."

"It is your community, too," a voice boomed from the back. A tall male, grey with age, made his way through the crowd.

"Hatos'Mok, Overseer of Lulnomia," Pan said. She took in his frame, older, frailer. Gone was much of the vitality he had possessed the last time she saw him. She wondered if the rift between him and Rohm'Mok had healed during her absence.

"No longer Overseer, I am afraid. That station passed to Irisa, daughter of Wrollonan'Tor, not long after you left."

Pan's eyes met his, and she waited.

The last time they had spoken, Hatos'Mok banished her from Lulnomia. A banishment she had dismissed, declaring that she answered to a higher authority than his. It was certainly not his welcome that she waited for. No. She needed no one's permission to return here. By her silence, she gave him the opportunity publicly to undo the great wrong he had committed against her. To cleanse himself of the shame he had brought on himself through his anger with her.

He spoke. "Welcome home, Pan, Guardian of Etera."

Relief rolled through the crowd. Though the community was made up of many who had been offling at the time Pan left Lulnomia, as well as those who had been born since, they had heard the story and knew of the time the Guardian Pan formed the Ror'Eckrah, removed the memories of the Akassa and the Sassen, and called forth the Wrak-Ayya, the Age of Shadows. And how the Overseer had nearly destroyed Lulnomia, and himself, by banishing Pan for fulfilling her duties as Guardian.

"Let me show you where you can stay," Irisa said, reaching her hand out in an invitation for Pan and Moart'Tor to follow her.

The crowd parted to make way for them, and Pan fought with all the strength the impulse to look over at Rohm'Mok. She could say nothing, fearing the answer to the question that had burned in her heart since the moment she left.

Irisa motioned for Moart'Tor to enter the first room they came to. "You may choose another in time, but I thought this one best for now because of its location within the heart of Lulnomia. Though we are one, we are also each part of our original communities, which occupy dedicated portions of this great space. Since you do not belong to any particular group, it is fitting that you reside here for now."

"I am sure this has been a great deal to take in," Pan said to him. "Take some time to relax and settle in, and I will be back to see you later. In time, you will learn the routine and start to feel more comfortable."

Pan watched Moart'Tor cautiously enter the space, and when he did not reappear, turned to Irisa, who led her on, past one familiar turn after the next, though the paths were deeply worn and the walls now smooth from the passing of the many Mothoc hands brushing the walls as they walked. As they continued, Pan became more and more surprised by the route they were taking, until finally, they stood outside the quarters of the Leader of the High Rocks.

"Rohm'Mok decided not to stay here, and it is the closest you have to any place that is familiar. You have resided so long with my father and me. I thought—"

The Guardian's heart ached. When, so long ago, she was the Leader of the High Rocks as well as the Guardian, this had been her home with Rohm'Mok and Tala. Pan realized that Irisa thought it would comfort her to be back in her own room. She pulled open the huge stone door that enclosed the past. She took a step inside and looked around.

It was just as it had been on the day she left. There were hide covers on the sleeping area, similar to those she and Rohm'Mok had for so many nights snuggled under together. And there, on a small stand on what had been her side of the sleeping mat, remained a small red rock. The red jasper Rohm'Mok had given her when she returned from the rebel camp. The one he said Ravu-Bahl had dropped in the snow in front of him as a reminder of the Great Spirit's loving care.

Pan looked down at the solitary gem and closed her eyes to the memories that came flooding back.

"Perhaps this was a mistake, Guardian. I am sorry." Irisa now stood next to her.

Pan shook her head and placed a hand on the old female's shoulder. "You meant well, I know." Then, high in the eastern corner, she noticed the 'Tor Leader's staff.

She gasped. "Why is the Leader's Staff here? Vel was appointed Leader."

"She accepted the Leader's Staff when you handed it to her, but soon afterward, she returned it."

"Then who has led Kthama all this time?"

"She and Rohm'Mok have ruled together, though she only accepted the Leadership temporarily. She said that you were and would always be the rightful Leader and that you would return someday. She wanted it to be here waiting for you when that day dawned."

Pan stepped over to it and ran her hand slowly

down the length of the staff. The outside was just as she remembered, worn down by being handled through the eons. She wondered how many times her father had stood looking at it just as she was now, reflecting on all it meant. And all it required.

The room had not been lived in, and from what Irisa said, apparently from the day she had left. So, where was Rohm'Mok? And Tala? She was grown; she must be paired herself.

"Rohm'Mok?" Pan dared to say, hoping Irisa would understand what she couldn't bring herself to ask.

"He moved out the day you left and never returned."

Pan turned her head away. She didn't want or need to hear any more. It was done. It was the price she had to pay. The sacrifice of being the Guardian.

"I am sorry I brought you to these quarters, Pan—" In a rare show of emotion, Irisa's voice broke. "Would you rather—"

A faint smile touched Pan's face. Irisa had become her friend thousands of years ago, and in the time she had lived with Irisa and her father, they had become even closer.

"No, it is what it is. I made my choices, and I cannot run from them any longer. The Order of Functions, in its infinite orchestration, has brought me here to face them at last."

Rohm'Mok and Vel were sitting together with Tala.

"She is my mother, the one you taught me about," Tala said quietly, looking down at her hands folded in her lap.

"Yes, she is. She is Pan, Guardian of Etera," Vel said, reaching out to lay her hand on Tala's.

"You always said she would return, Father. You never stopped believing that."

"She said she would return, but I expected it would be with the Promised One. It is a surprise to see her bringing one of the rebels instead."

"Not just one of the rebels," Vel added. "The son of Dak'Tor, her brother, and mine."

"I wonder if she has learned what became of him. After Dak'Tor betrayed her and ran off, she seldom spoke of him. It was as if she simply separated out that part of her life and locked it away. I wonder if, because of this Moart'Tor, she now knows where he is—if he is even alive. I hope we soon learn of his fate."

"Despite all you have told me of my mother, she has remained a mystery. I want to get to know her." Tala moved over to rest her hand on her father's shoulder.

"I know, and it is my fervent prayer that you will be given the chance to do just that. I hope she will stay now that she has returned, but there is no way of knowing."

Tala turned her head to look at Vel. "Mother, you understand? Please tell me you understand that I do not want to replace you with her."

"Of course I do. Love is not a divider; it is a multiplier. You must not trouble yourself with my feelings. For one thing, there is no need. Pan is my sister, and I have missed her more than I can say. That she has returned home is a miracle and a great blessing. I am secure in my place in your heart. You can love both of us in different ways." Vel ran her hand down the back of Tala's hair, stroking it gently.

"I am a grown female, acting like this," Tala said, wiping tears with the back of her arm. But even after so very many years, suddenly, Tala did not feel grown. She felt like the young offling she had been, the one who longed for her mother, who had cried tears alone in the dark for the one who had abandoned her—the person whose name she had called out in her dreams but who never returned.

Vel had been a wonderful mother, and nothing could change that. But how to live with this now? How to relate to Pan in the vacuum of any shared experiences between them? Whatever relationship there would be, beyond a name, they would have to build it together. But Tala wondered if there would be time to do just that. Or would Pan slip off again to—wherever she had been the entire time Tala was growing up?

Pan collapsed onto the sleeping mat and stretched out. She wanted to go home. Home to the life she had built with Irisa and Wrollonan'Tor, only she could not. She must stay here. She must see it through, however hard it was.

She thought of the world she had created using the methods Wrollonan'Tor had taught her. First, it had been a little enclosure woven from thick vines, the inside floor covered in rich green moss. It was a place of comfort and solace, and she quickly became enamored with it. As her powers grew and she realized how to use them to mold the world around her—the dimension in which she lived with Wrollonan'Tor and Irisa—her little shelter had become larger, more spacious. But it never lost its warm and comforting qualities.

Eventually, pink and purple blossoms bloomed inside and out, and openings would appear in the woven vines once it was dark so she could glimpse the stars overhead. Occasionally, a red fox would appear and curl up against her in the crook of her knees or around the top of her head. Other times, it would be a huge grey wolf who would lie up against her back. They always seemed to come when she needed them most, and they helped ease the loneliness that attended some of her nights.

But this time, no one would come to comfort her.

Not fox, deer, or wolf. Or mate. Her fears had come to pass, and she realized how much she had unconsciously believed that Rohm'Mok would have waited for her. She wondered how long she would have to stay at Lulnomia. It was one thing to live in Wrollonan'Tor's world, the reality he had created, which was just a vibration out of sync with the rest of Etera. There, in the centuries she had spent with him and Irisa, Pan was able to put Lulnomia out of her mind—for the most part. She supposed it was because not knowing had kept the dream alive, the dream that when she did return, her beloved would be waiting for her as he had said he would be.

That dream was now dead.

Pan got up and paced about the room. The decision was not hers to make, but she knew she would, at the very least, have to stay long enough to get Moart'Tor rooted in the community. He was no threat, and not just because he was no longer the towering behemoth dominating everyone and everything around him. Here, he was one of a thousand males, perhaps a bit more robust in build than many and with striking coloring, but nonetheless, he could not wreak havoc here. If he tried anything, he would immediately be overcome.

But she didn't expect trouble from Moart'Tor. If she had, she would never have brought him to Lulnomia. She knew his shame was genuine and that he did truly want a chance at redemption to right the wrongs he had committed or had planned to commit. And she firmly believed everyone deserved a second chance.

She ended up back in front of the Leader's Staff, reached out, wrapped her hand around it, and stood there, silent. How familiar it felt under her fingers. How it seemed to mold itself to her grip, almost like an embrace. She gave it a sharp pull and popped it out of the recess she had carved in the rock wall for its safekeeping.

Where it had been perfectly balanced before, it was now off. Of course, the crystal her father had stored in the top piece was gone, taken by Dak'Tor, though she did not know why. Because he felt it had some value for barter or trade? Because he believed he could learn to harness its power? Or simply out of spite? Their father had picked him to be Leader, not her. Dak'Tor was the one to whom Moc'Tor had entrusted the knowledge of the crystal. And what of the scroll Lor Onida had created during the time of her father's Guardianship, which all had thought lost? Had Moc'Tor also told her brother about Lor Onida's scroll?

It did no good to think about these things. At some point, she would travel to the rebel camp, and then, just as it had come to pass here, she would have the answers that at least part of her did not want.

Lulnomia was abuzz with talk about the Guardian's return. At any point along the tunnels and in the community rooms, there were small clusters of Mothoc talking among themselves.

Before Pan had introduced the male with her, for a moment, many had thought he was the Promised One, though others rightly argued that the Guardian had not said she would return only with the Promised One. In the end, they were satisfied to learn that he was the son of Dak'Tor. Not as interesting, but it still provided a great deal of mystery to speculate about.

However, mostly, they talked about Rohm'Mok and Pan. That Pan had promised to return and that he had promised to wait for her. Would she stay at Lulnomia now, or would she soon leave again?

After Pan had left, the community went through a period of great turmoil. Many of them sided with Pan and her decision to invoke the Ror'Eckrah, while others agreed with Hatos'Mok that she had overstepped her authority. And yet, as she had said, she answered to the authority of the Great Spirit, not to the Overseer or the High Council. Back and forth it had gone, and the debate continued for hundreds of years until enough time had passed that it just didn't seem important any longer. What truly mattered was that the Guardian had given up everything she loved —her beloved, her daughter, her sisters, her place among her own kind—to do what she believed she had to do. And it was not just for her sake; it was for the sake of everyone.

In the end, humility won out as each questioned their own ability to sacrifice what she had, and any animosity toward the Guardian passed into the streams of time.

Though Pan and the other Leaders had thought that eventually, the delineation of the living areas would break down, they had not. The communities remained as they were first assigned, and the community identity was defined by the locations the Mothoc had lived in before coming to Lulnomia. It was a peaceful co-existence, but the Lulnomia identity Hatos'Mok had spoken of when he was Overseer was still not where he had dreamed it would be.

Before she left, Pan had realized that Lor'Onida's scroll might be the unifying factor, yet she did not reveal its existence. A check in her spirit held her back. She knew it was the fact that the rebel Mothoc were still estranged. She still held out hope that they could be brought back into the fold, and then they would truly be united again.

Her father, the Guardian Moc'Tor, had never wanted this division. It was never any part of his plan, and yet, in the end, it had to happen to protect the Akassa and to preserve as much of the Mothoc blood as possible in the Sassen. How peculiar that, oftentimes, the wisdom of a path walked can only be seen in retrospect. Each step appears and is taken in faith, but later you could turn around and see where it had been leading and the wisdom behind it.

Pan was not ready to face Vel, but she sought out her other sister.

Inrion embraced Pan warmly. “My heart leaps with joy that you have returned home to us.”

Pan savored the contact and let herself absorb every moment.

Admiring her sister’s appearance, Inrion said, “You have not changed, but I know I have.”

“You are a mature female now, in all your glory,” Pan replied. “Tell me about your life.”

“I have a mate and two offling, a son and a daughter, both grown. We are very happy together. He is from the Far High Hills community, and I moved there with him. He is very close to his family, and they have been nothing but kind and accepting.”

Pan inwardly cringed, wondering if that meant there had been repercussions from her own behavior that had affected her sister. “Did you have problems with the community after I created the Ror’Eckrah?”

“I thought I might; both Vel and I did.”

At Vel’s name, Pan dropped her eyes for a moment.

Inrion continued, “But there were as many people upset with Hatos’Mok for banishing you—well, trying to banish you—as there were with you for doing what you did. Over time, almost everyone decided that he had overstepped his authority as Overseer. He relinquished the position not too long after, even though Irisa had counseled him not to, and she was elected Overseer in his place. It was the best move, really. Being the daughter of a Guardian, Irisa helped those who were still upset with you to realize your responsibilities come from a higher source."

"I have missed so much," Pan lamented.

"Have you—spoken with Vel?"

"No, other than seeing her with Rohm'Mok when I arrived. I have not spoken to either of them."

Inrion put her hand on Pan's arm. "You need to speak with them. Please."

"I am not ready. I will, though, I promise. If they do not seek me out, I will not let it go on forever. I know I have to face the truth."

"Yes, you do," Inrion said gently. "For everyone's sake, please do not let too much time pass."

Having gathered her thoughts, Pan decided it was time to address the entire community. After Irisa had arranged an assembly, the Guardian went to find Moart'Tor.

He stood when she arrived at his quarters. "Come in." With a sweep of his hand, he invited her to sit down.

"I wanted to give us both some time," Pan said.

"Thank you. It is a lot to absorb that this community exists, that there are so many Mothoc—and so many offling."

"And you only saw a portion of the community when we arrived. I will be addressing everyone tomorrow evening, and I wanted you to know. I thought I would now take you on a tour to start your adjustment to living here."

"Am I welcome here, even though I am part of what everyone calls the rebel group?"

"I would not have brought you here otherwise. The Mothoc want unity, and your people would be welcome here. It is still my fervent hope that this will happen, but it is only possible if their attitudes toward the Akassa and the Sassen are changed."

"As mine was. It is one thing to hate an idea or a faceless group, but living among the Sassen for even that short time and observing what I did at the assembly at the Far High Hills—it changed everything."

"That was possible in your situation because, as one individual, you were not a threat to the Sassen. It is not possible for all of Zuenerth to have the same experience, so we must reach them some other way, though I do not yet know what that will be," Pan remarked.

"There are many there who would welcome living here, I am sure of it."

"Ah, but how to separate them out from those

who cannot relinquish the hatred from their hearts? That is a problem. And their motivation must not just be to live here among the rest of their kind; their hearts must truly be cleansed of the desire to annihilate the Akassa and the Sassen."

"Whatever I can do to help, Guardian, I pledge to you my fealty."

Pan looked into Moart'Tor's eyes for quite some time. He met her gaze steadily, and she knew he was being honest.

Moart'Tor then said, "May I ask you a personal question?"

Pan nodded, so he continued, "When we arrived, there was a male who, with your sisters, broke from the crowd and greeted you. What is he to you?"

"He was my mate. We bore a daughter together, and I had to leave them behind to fulfill my duty as Guardian."

"You said *was*—"

"Yes. We were paired at Kthama before we came here. It is a long story, Moart'Tor, but to answer your question, he was everything to me. As my daughter was."

"We know so little of the Guardians, and in that emptiness, we have come to our own conclusions. I thought of your life as one only of entitlement, and I resented you for being set above the rest of us. Now, I am beginning to see the other side. The station of Guardian also brings great responsibility, and in a way, your life is not your own."

Pan was touched by his insight. "You are correct. It was one of the hardest lessons I have had to learn—and accept. The day-to-day blessings that are afforded to all others and so easily taken for granted are given to me only as a privilege—and often a temporary one at that. I paid dearly for the choices I have had to make, as did my father, Moc'Tor, and his brother."

"And the one you call Wrollonan'Tor?"

"He was the Guardian before my father, although they were only very distant relations. The story was that he had died, but in truth, he had simply left so my father could become Guardian of Etera."

"He seems as old as time itself," Moart'Tor said almost absent-mindedly.

"I had the same impression when I first met him. Ancient. I do not know how long he has lived, and I wonder if he possibly also does not know. He, too, has made tremendous sacrifices."

Sadness fell over Pan. The Guardian's mantle had cost Moc'Tor everything, too. Only he was not in the Corridor in the arms of her mother, E'ranale. His soul was trapped in the vortex, in the Order of Functions, splintered and stretched to infinity, his life on Etera sacrificed in service to the Great Spirit. She wondered if she would have been strong enough to do what she had to do if her father had not entered the vortex to help her. Wrollonan'Tor had been with her, but without her father's support from within the Order of Functions, would the two of them have been able to form the Ror'Eckrah, which freed the Akassa and Sassen from their memories of their Protectors?

She prayed that someday she would be able to ask him these questions. She knew what it was like to merge with the Order of Functions. Over the thousands of years, she had built up a resistance to the experience, an ability to bear it, but part of that was knowing it was only temporary and that soon she would enter the Aezaiteran stream and be soothed by the healing balm of that pure creative force. For her father, however, there was no guarantee he would ever be freed. It was a terrible thought, and she did not allow her thoughts to go there often. She knew only that the crystal was part of the key to freeing him. The crystal. What had Dak'Tor done with the crystal?

Over the years, Dak'Tor and his family and followers had kept their personal beliefs to themselves, giving the appearance of supporting Kaisak's mission to exterminate the Akassa and the Sassen. If it could be made known, Dak'Tor estimated that the community would probably be split almost evenly, half agreeing with Kaisak and the other half secretly not. Only in the most hushed and private of settings did he and other like-minded individuals speak of what they would do if Kaisak decided to go to war against the Akassa and the Sassen.

The Leader needed more information about what they would be up against, and for that, he had sent Moart'Tor to Kayerm.

What Kaisak did not know was that the Mothoc were no longer living with either the Akassa or the Sassen. At least, Dak'Tor believed Pan had followed through and led all the Mothoc to some place they had named Lulnomia, which raised the stakes for any attack Kaisak might launch. But Kaisak continued to believe that, in all the communities, the Mothoc still lived beside the Akassa and Sassen. If Moart'Tor returned and the rebel Leader learned from him that the Sassen and the Akassa were no longer under the direct protection of the Mothoc, that could change everything.

But the future of Etera depended on every drop of blood of the remaining Mothoc and Sassen.

Kaisak had planned all along for Moart'Tor at some point to try and find the Sassen, to learn all he could about them. How many they were, if they had the same breeding challenges that his own community at Zuenerth was now facing, and anything at all about the Promised One. The original Leader of the rebels, Laborn, had dismissed the Guardian and her powers, as well as her proclamation of the coming of the Promised One, but where Laborn had not believed the Guardians had any special abilities, Kaisak was not so sure. If nothing else, the mystery and lack of information about Etera's Guardians had turned them into legend. And that in itself gave them power and influence.

Though Moart'Tor's blood father was Dak'Tor, as an offling, he had been raised by Kaisak and Moart'Tor's mother, Visha. Therefore, his parental relationship was with Kaisak, and so, Dak'Tor had to assume, was his allegiance. So Dak'Tor had never spoken with Moart'Tor about his disagreement with the rebel Leader's cause of eliminating the Sassen and the Akassa. He could not take the chance.

But Moart'Tor had been gone longer than either Kaisak or Visha had projected, and Visha was openly disturbed about it. Though the Leader had moved his quarters away from the main community dwellings, Visha's voice carried, so many knew of her frustration and anger at her mate's not being more concerned.

Dak'Tor had never been worried for Moart'Tor's safety. He knew that even if the Sassen did not believe him, they would not harm him. If by some chance, they realized why he had truly sought them out, there would not be much they could do. In their position, he was not sure what action he would take. If they meant to detain him as punishment, it would be a lifetime sentence, but Moart'Tor would still be safe.

If it were Kaisak who had discovered an outsider integrating into his community under the pretense of looking for sanctuary, Dak'Tor had no doubt the intruder would be killed. And probably publicly.

It was late, and Dak'Tor and his mate had settled in for the night.

"I feel sorry for Visha," Iria said. Though it was springtime, the weather was still cool enough at night to make snuggling enjoyable, and she nestled in closer against her mate. "She is truly worried about Moart'Tor."

"I do not think he is in any danger, but I do wonder what has happened to him. It is possible he never found Kayerm, though unlikely. It is also possible he simply decided to stay and live with the Sassen, though that is also unlikely, considering how Kaisak has poisoned his mind against them. If he did not find Kayerm, at some point, he would have given up and retraced his steps, in which case, he should still have been back by now. So, yes, it is a mystery."

"What about the outcome you did not mention that you perhaps did not want to think possible?"

"That he died on the way? That some mishap befell him?" Dak'Tor shook his head. "It seems unlikely. He is in his prime, filled with strength and vitality. So all we have are equally unlikely possibilities."

"And yet one of them must be true."

"Either he cannot return, or he does not want to. Both seem implausible, so we will just have to wait. Kaisak will not send anyone after him, I am sure of that."

"Kaisak was counting on him bringing back information, especially about the Promised One," Iria said. "I wonder what he will do now. Do you think, if Kaisak were gone, that those who believe as he does would pick up the cause?"

"In those our age, he has instilled the belief that the Sassen and the Akassa are an abomination. As for the offling, I do not know where their allegiance lies. They have no personal experience of the time we lived through. Perhaps without his keeping it alive, the animosity might fade."

"You do not think his other sons would carry the fight on his behalf?"

"I am not sure. Probably not without a personal reason. None of them seems very motivated by anything except being allocated a female. Perhaps, if it turned out the Sassen did harm to Moart'Tor— But I cannot imagine that in any way, nor if it did happen, how we would hear of it and how it could be proven."

"We have lived a good life regardless." Iria looked up to meet her mate's eyes.

"Yes, we have. I love you with all my heart, and that will never change. Though I wish I could have taken you from here. I wish I could have given you a life elsewhere, one free from this spirit of bitterness Kaisak contaminates the community with." He kissed the top of her forehead.

"We have done our best to shield our offling from it, and they are as happy and well adjusted as any could be here. I am only sad that they are not living the life we have shared—being permitted to pair and have offling of their own."

"They have each other and their friends, and I am proud that they all get along so well. But nothing takes the place of a mate, I know." Dak'Tor pulled her a little bit closer, and before he fell asleep, said a prayer for Moart'Tor.

CHAPTER 4

It had been a long journey, made longer by traveling alone, but, despite being lonely, Newell Storis had not been bored. He had a million thoughts running through his mind about the Brothers' predicament and also about the Akassa and the Sassen. He had been given a glimpse of an unimaginable world, and it had fractured his confidence that these two peoples could exist in the world he thought he knew. After all, if such people existed unbeknownst to the rest of Etera, what other secrets might there be?

He also pondered the story he would tell Grace and her family. He hated to lie, but in this case, there was no other choice. He would leave out the Akassa and the Sassen, and it would be lying by omission, but that was still a lie. It gave him even deeper compassion for Grayson Morgan, for the challenges life had handed him.

He would be home by evening. He assumed his wife, Grace, was staying with her parents as he had asked, and he was anxious to hold her in his arms again.

Newell knocked and heard Buster and Grace's puppy, Pippy, rushing to the door.

After a moment, Nora opened it. "Newell!"

Grace appeared behind her. "You're home!" she exclaimed as she rushed into his arms.

Joyfully, he caught her up in his embrace. "I'm home," he said, his words muffled.

While Newell was embracing his wife, Nora stepped past them. "Ned, where is Ned? Is he not with you?"

By now, Matthew had joined them. "Welcome home, Newell. Did he not come back?"

Newell let go of Grace. "Ned is with Grayson. It is what he wants, and he is safe and happy. Here." He reached into his jacket pocket. "These are for you and Matthew, and this one's for you, Grace." He handed them the letters Ned had written.

"I assure you, he is fine. And even though he changed his mind once before, this time, there is no question about it. He has found his place in the world, and he is at peace."

Seeing their faces, Newell quickly added, "He as

much as promised that he will come home next spring if there is any way possible."

Nora's face lit up somewhat at that news. "Come and sit down; we were just starting to eat." She led him to the kitchen.

Newell closed his eyes and took in the smell of the hearty stew, warm biscuits, and seasoned green beans. He knew he would eat more than he should but made up his mind not to regret it one bit. He took a seat next to his wife and grasped her hand.

"How are you, honey," he asked Grace.

"I'm fine, Newell. Everything is going well, and staying here has made it a lot easier on me, that is for sure."

"But I know you will be glad to get home to your little yellow cottage," Nora said as she plopped another scoop of stew onto Newell's plate.

Grace good-humoredly rolled her eyes at the large helping, to which Newell laughed and dug in anyway.

"Forgive me, but I have lived primarily on roots, shoots, and unidentified meat for the past few months. I had forgotten how great a cook you are, Nora," he said before shoveling another helping into his mouth. He was reveling in being back in the familiar, cozy Webb kitchen.

"Are you too tired to talk about what happened?" Nora asked. "I understand if you are."

"Perhaps I should give you the details another time,

but we did find Chief Kotori's people and got them safely back home. Many of them were exhausted, and some of the elderly were very sick. It was a harrowing experience, and it was a miracle we found them."

"What had happened?" Matthew asked.

"The Governor sent a regiment to take them from their home. They were being driven through the snow to a military outpost, and when enough locals were gathered, they were to be moved out west. It was all about taking their land."

He swallowed another bite and added, "Which is ludicrous to them, as they do not believe anyone can own the land."

"So the fact that Grayson had bought the land they were on is what made the difference?" Matthew asked.

"Yes. Exactly. Once the regiment commander saw the paperwork, he immediately turned them over to us. I think he was glad to do it. We found them just before they got to the outpost, not that it would have mattered; we would have tracked them down there."

Finally, the question Newell had been dreading came up. "Did you see Ben and Miss Vivian?" Grace asked.

He hadn't intended on admitting to it, but in the end, he knew they were legitimately concerned, so he told them. He then told them about Oh'Dar's daughter, I'Layah, and her surprising coloring. But he also explained that, out of respect for Oh'Dar's wishes, he could not go into where they were living and added that he now understood why Oh'Dar was willing to die rather than reveal their location.

"You are presenting a huge mystery," Nora said. "I know you can't talk about it, but it just makes it all that much more interesting."

"All I can do is ask for your understanding and your trust that if I could tell you, I would. Think of it as attorney-client privilege. Maybe that will make it easier to accept."

"Oddly enough, that does," Nora said. "It makes it less personal, more about a boundary to be respected."

Newell set his fork down. "Oh, I have to stop eating. It is delicious, but if I don't stop now, I won't sleep tonight, and I am so looking forward to sleeping in a real bed. The everyday things we take for granted! I must also see properly to the horses."

"You and Grace are welcome to stay here as long as you wish, but if you want to go to your own home, we certainly understand," Matthew said.

"If it is all the same to you and Grace, I would just as soon stay here. Our house will be cold, and I am not up to getting the fire and hearth started tonight."

Matthew got up from the table. "Come; I will help you as much as I can."

"As soon as the dishes are done and put away, Newell, Grace and I will prepare you a warm bath. How does that sound?" Nora volunteered.

"You read my mind. Thank you very much!"

Newell had been wrong. He had thought there was nothing better than the stew, warm biscuits, and butter, and yet here he was, soaking in bliss. The warmth soothed his muscles, and the fragrance of the soapy water wafted his cares away. It was all he could do not to fall asleep in the tub. Grace kept heating water so he could stay in as long as he wanted, and only the promise of curling up next to his wife lured him out of the luxurious bath. Nora gave Grace a clean set of Matthew's sleepwear so Newell could be as comfortable as possible.

With the bath over, Newell went upstairs and slipped between the soft sheets. The mattress molded itself to his body, and he let out a long sigh. He looked at the ceiling, the walls, and the nightstand next to the bed. All these things were, for the most part, mundane against the backdrop of day-to-day existence, yet, tonight, each one seemed like a luxury befitting a king.

He lay in bed, waiting for Grace to join him. Buster was curled up at his feet, head resting on one of his ankles, and Newell enjoyed the weight of the little body next to him. Even the amazing loyalty and comfort of a little dog was a great gift, the appreciation of which was so easily lost among the tyranny of the day's demands.

Newell heard soft footsteps coming up the stairs,

so he turned on his side and pushed himself back to the wall, making room for Grace.

"Forgive me for going to bed ahead of you," he said as she entered. Pippy followed her into the room, his nails clicking across the wood floor, and curled up on a rug in the corner.

Grace closed the door behind her, turned the oil lamp down, and slipped in next to him. "There's no need to apologize. It makes no sense for you to stand around waiting for me to finish down oil lamp there when you could be up here relaxing after your journey. I know it has been a hard trip. I can see it in your face."

Newell brushed a golden lock from her forehead. "Are you sure everything is alright?"

"Yes. It is." Grace fixed her green eyes on him. "I know you are exhausted, so just sleep, my love. Having you home safe and sound is more than enough for tonight."

The truth was, Newell was exhausted, but he didn't want to sleep. Not with his beautiful curvy wife in his arms once again. But, in the end, the exhaustion won out. The lavender scent of her hair was sending him off to dreamland, and within moments, he was fast asleep.

The next morning, they moved back to their little yellow house. Newell borrowed Matthew's wagon and loaded up Grace's belongings, including Pippy. The goats had been moved to the Webbs' farm along with Grace and were tied up behind.

Once Newell had the goats secured in their old pen and Grace had taken inventory of what was needed in the house, he took her into town to get supplies. Soon after they returned, he had a roaring fire going in the hearth as well as in the living room fireplace.

"You are back in time for us to plant the spring garden," Grace said. Her head was resting on Newell's shoulder as they relaxed on the couch.

"I will take care of it; you just tell me where you want things, and I'll do the rest. Being back home makes me realize how much I have taken for granted. Our life together, your family, the comforts we are blessed with—and being warm all over at once."

She turned to look at her husband. "It sounds as if you had quite an experience, and I am so happy you are home. But what will now happen with Ned?"

There had been lots of time for Newell to anticipate probable questions to figure out which he could answer and which he would have to dodge.

"Ned is going to learn the locals' language and culture more thoroughly, and then he will travel from village to village and teach them English."

"Why in the world would they want to know how to— Oh, of course. It would help the locals deal with the soldiers if there was another attempt at abduction."

"Yes, and the locals could understand what is being said, even if they didn't want to let it be known," Newell answered. "In my heart, I don't think the relocation of the locals will stop, I'm sorry to say."

"And Grayson?"

"Grayson has to meet with the Governor. I know it is the last thing he wants to do, but he is convinced the Governor didn't know that the locals were taken from private land and wants to make sure he gets the message, loud and clear."

Newell was right. The last thing Oh'Dar wanted was to go and see the Governor, but he knew he had to. Right now, he was shackled by responsibilities. Much like his mother, Adia, who longed for her days to settle down into routine, Oh'Dar longed for the time he could just be a parent, grandson, and life-walker.

Oh'Dar knew Adia would soon be home at Kthama, and he told Acise, Ned, Ben, and his grandmother that he was leaving to see the Governor so he could put that behind him and hopefully be back by the time his mother returned.

Oh'Dar said his goodbyes, and with the Morgan Trust papers safely in a coat pocket, he and Storm set out through the cool weather to find the Governor.

Governor Wright's secretary led Oh'Dar into an expensively decorated office. An oversized carved walnut desk dominated the room, and along the walls were wooden columns with busts of historical figures atop them. The oil lamps had little crystals dangling from their mounts. Heavy brocade curtains, running nearly floor to ceiling, added to the elegant theme. The opulence struck Oh'Dar as overdone, surpassing even his grandmother's taste for finery back at Shadow Ridge.

The Governor rose to his feet and came around from behind the huge desk. "Hello, Mr. Morgan. You are the great-grandson of Grayson Stone Morgan, are you not? To what do I owe the pleasure of this visit?"

"Yes, sir, I am, and I am sure you know the story behind my parents' murder."

"Yes, well, it is a very well-known story, a terrible thing. I knew your grandfather fairly well, and I was sorry when he passed. I understand your grandmother re-married, though."

"Yes. The farm manager whom my grandfather hired when he and my grandmother were first married."

"I am glad she found happiness again. What can I do for you, Mr. Morgan?" Governor Wright asked.

"I have recently come from intercepting one of your regiments in their abduction of a tribe of locals."

"Intercepting? Abduction? What do you mean?"

"Those people were taken away from their homes by a Commander Riley. They were nearly at the commander's outpost by the time I tracked them down," Oh'Dar explained.

"The commander was acting on my orders. I am sure you realize that the government has a responsibility to make the best use of government-owned land."

Oh'Dar reached inside and took out the packet of papers. "The property they were on is owned by the Morgan Trust. Those people were abducted from private land."

"May I?" The Governor reached for the papers. He opened the packet and studied them for a moment before folding them up again and handing them back to Oh'Dar. "I was not aware of this, I assure you. Constable Riggs carried my orders to the outpost. I will make sure he is aware of this so no others are removed from your land."

"Constable Riggs?"

"Yes. You know him?" The Governor raised his eyebrows.

"Governor, surely you are aware of the trial that just concluded, one in which I was accused of murdering my grandmother and her husband, Ben Jenkins."

"Yes, I heard of it. I am pleased they found you not guilty and that your grandmother and Mr. Jenkins are well."

"Did you not know that Constable Riggs was involved in having me charged with murder?"

"Yes. What bearing does that have on this matter?"

"Not long after the trial ended, the constable showed up at the closest village to us and told the Chief there that they had to vacate their land—and that if they didn't, he would come and do it for them. At that time, I showed him proof that all the surrounding land was now owned by the Morgan Trust. After that, he arrived at the village with the intent to remove several of the women there and their children as they were part white, and he told the locals he was acting under your orders. He and his men pulled guns on the Chief and his people."

Oh'Dar could have sworn Governor Wright's ruddy face turned a little pale.

The man walked away and stood behind his desk. "I assure you, Mr. Morgan, I knew nothing of Constable Riggs' actions."

Oh'Dar tightened his lips. "He claimed he was acting on your order, both times."

"The only action he took under my authority was to deliver my sealed order to the commander of the outpost where the locals were being collected." The Governor put his hand on the back of his chair, his knuckles turning white.

"Very well. I trust there will be no further trouble from Constable Riggs? Or, for that matter, from anyone else regarding the people living on Morgan Trust land."

"No. I can give you my assurance there will not

be. But, Mr. Morgan," he continued, "you cannot protect all the locals. And now that I am aware you have been purchasing land, I can assure you there will be no more land sales to the Morgan Trust. The relocation of these people *is* going to happen, and I suggest you make peace with it."

"I will never make peace with it, as you say, Governor. You are on the wrong side of this situation. These people were here first; we are the intruders, and the condition I found them in, under the care of your military, was despicable. It is a miracle none of them died. So if there is anything I can do to stop this travesty, I give you my assurance that I will do so. Thank you for your time." Without being dismissed, Oh'Dar tucked his papers back into his breast pocket and left, firmly closing the huge double doors behind him.

What Oh'Dar could not see behind those doors was the Governor, in a rage, sweeping everything off the top of his desk. Oh'Dar was also by then too far away to hear him storm out of the office and bark at his secretary, "Find Constable Riggs and get him here. Now!"

Riggs was in his cousin's office when the messenger showed up with an order to report to the Governor right away.

Sheriff Boone looked at Riggs. "That doesn't sound good. What have you done now, Samuel?"

"I haven't done anything. I have no idea what this is about. Perhaps it is good news."

"In my experience, anything containing the words *right away* is not good news."

Several days later, Riggs was in the same waiting room that Oh'Dar had been in a week or so before. The secretary opened the doors leading into the gubernatorial office.

Riggs removed his hat and held it in front of him. "You sent for me, Governor Wright?"

"Did you deliver my last order to the commander of the outpost, as I asked?"

"Yes, I did, sir. Is there a problem?"

"There is. It turns out that those people were living on private land."

Riggs stiffened, his hands now fiercely clutching his hat and unconsciously starting to twist it.

"Do you have nothing to say about this?"

"Governor, I—"

The Governor slammed his palm down on his walnut desk. "Dammit, Riggs. You knew that was private land. You knew the land was owned by the Morgan Trust and that those orders were illegal, and you didn't say anything to me about it. Why not?"

Riggs could not think of a thing to say in his defense.

"Oh, and there's more. I understand you also visited the Morgan village and pulled a gun on their Chief and several others. And you said you were there on my authority to remove some of them because they were of mixed blood?" The Governor stared at Riggs, waiting for an answer but knowing none would be coming.

"I entrusted you with a powerful station, Riggs. A hundred men would give their eye teeth to be my Constable of Territories, and you abused that trust and that station and created a public relations nightmare for me. In an election year!" The Governor glared at the constable a moment longer, then fixed his gaze meaningfully on the silver badge on Riggs' chest.

Understanding, Riggs slowly reached up and removed his badge. He placed it gently on the Governor's desk.

"I expect never to see you again, Mr. Riggs. And if there are long-standing repercussions, this will not be the end of it between you and me. And for God's sake, I strongly suggest you stay out of anything to do with the Morgans."

Riggs wasn't sure how the Governor had found out about the Morgan Trust, but he was sure Grayson

Morgan was involved. Knowing that word traveled slowly, and fueled by his anger, he rode directly to the outpost and demanded to see the commander.

"Bringing more orders from the Governor, Constable?" Commander Riley asked.

"No, just checking up on the last one, though. You have had more than enough time to collect the locals from the first village; where are they being held?"

"They're not. We were almost back here when a man named Grayson Stone Morgan the Third showed up. He produced papers that proved that the village we took them from was on private property. We surrendered them to his care."

"I see," Riggs said, not wanting to give away any information. "Did you alert the Governor?"

"No. You said you would return, so I waited for you. I thought you would want to tell him yourself."

"Thank you, Commander Riley. I will be sure to let him know."

Riggs was fuming. It *was* Morgan who had told the Governor. He didn't know how yet, but he was going to exact payment for this. Morgan had cost him a very influential position, one that would never in his lifetime come his way again. Now, what was he supposed to do? When word of this got out, and it eventually would, no one anywhere near would hire him. How was he to support himself? The position had afforded him a very comfortable lifestyle.

Not knowing what to do, Riggs headed for his

sister's place in Appleton. He needed a place to hide and think this through. He was overdue for a visit anyway.

Riggs removed his hat and stepped inside the modest farmhouse. It was simply appointed but still had a sense of charm to it. It had been some time since he had visited, but almost everything was as he remembered it.

He followed his sister, Mary, to a little sitting room.

"Sit here, please," she insisted. "It's the most comfortable chair."

Riggs sat down. "I thought I was overdue for a visit. At our great uncle's funeral in Braxton, we didn't take enough time to talk."

"Well, yes; it has been a long time. Are you well; is something wrong? You look peaked—if you don't mind my saying. Wait here; I'll bring you a cup of hot tea."

He took the cup she returned with and waited as she sat across from him on a wooden rocking chair.

"Now, please, tell me. What is it?"

Riggs wanted to tell her the truth, but he was ashamed. "I just wanted to check on you and John. How is the farm coming along?"

"Fine. Fine. Last year was dry, and we worried we

would lose our crops, but we made it. It's always touch and go, as you know."

Riggs did know all about that life. He and his sister had suffered through it while growing up. It was one of the reasons he had vowed never to be a farmer; there were too many things that could go wrong. In addition, you had to have a family if you had a farm, and he had never made time to settle down.

"Mary, I thought, if it is not a burden, I might stay with you and John for a while. I can help out with the chores."

"You are welcome here, of course. But it's unusual for the Governor to give you time off like this," she frowned.

"I'm not working for the Governor anymore." Riggs got up and paced a little. "I don't know what I'm going to do. When word gets out that the Governor fired me, my name will be ruined. I'm not sure what to do next."

"I see," Mary said, her voice soft. "I'm sorry, Sam. I know how hard you worked to get that position. Do you want to tell me about it?"

"Not much to tell. I delivered some orders from the Governor to start removals of the locals from government land. Turned out that the first group the outpost picked up was on private property. The Governor blamed me for not knowing."

"That doesn't seem fair."

"It wasn't. The owner of the land is one of the

Morgans. He has a grudge against me because I was involved in his trial for the murder of his grandmother and her husband. He was found innocent but still blames me for the trouble. I was just doing my job. But he went to the Governor and told him I knew it was private land."

"I heard about the trial," Mary commented.

"The Morgans are very powerful, always have been, so who is the Governor going to side with? His wealthy cohorts, of course. He said something about it being an election year."

"You can stay here as long as you need to, Sam, you know that."

Mary stood up and laid a hand on his arm. "I need to tend to dinner. Do you want to clean up? Did you bring your things?"

"They're outside; I'll get them. Thank you."

Mary patted his arm again and went into the kitchen.

While Riggs was upstairs washing up, Mary's husband, John, came in. "We have company?" He hung his hat on a peg by the door and then stooped over to remove his muddy work boots.

"Yes, my brother. He ran into some trouble and needs to stay with us a bit."

"Is everything alright?"

"The Governor fired him over what he says was a misunderstanding, so he needs someplace to collect his thoughts about what to do next."fired

John kissed Mary on the forehead. "He's welcome here, of course. He's your brother."

"Thank you. I know he's not the easiest person to have around."

"We'll make do."

After supper, when Mary and John's boys were upstairs, Riggs went over his story again. John listened carefully but didn't ask many questions.

Later, when he and Mary were in bed, John said, "Something doesn't add up."

Mary sighed. "I know."

"I don't rightly know the Governor, but I do know your brother. I'm sorry to say, but if someone is in the wrong here, I'm afraid I would bet on it being Sam."

"That also occurred to me. He isn't telling us the whole story, but I didn't want to put him on the spot; he seems so—hopeless."

"It wouldn't be the first time he's twisted his stories to his benefit. At some point, we'll need to know the truth. But I understand. He's family, and we can't just abandon him now."

"I've seen him in a state before, but this is a new one. Thank you for understanding."

The next morning, John showed Samuel around the farm again, pointing out things that needed fixing. "You used to be a pretty good carpenter, as I remember," he said.

"I can still do some stuff, sure. Your fences look like they could use some work."

"Always. You know about that; you and Mary grew up on the farm. The work never stops. The boys help when they get out of school, but we can always use an extra hand. We always need wood chopped. And, depending on how long you stay, spring planting's upon us, and we can always use an extra hand at harvest time, I'm sure you remember."

"I hope I'm not here that long. Well, you know what I mean."

"Of course," John said.

Riggs started walking the fence line to see where it most needed work. He would tackle the fixing right away. He needed the time alone, and the fresh air would help clear his mind. For the first time in a long time, he truly didn't know what to do. In the back of his mind, he feared he might have to move far away. He wasn't cut out to be a farmer, and he wasn't going to go back to that life. He needed a job where he didn't have to get his hands dirty, but no one would want to go against the Governor—and even maybe not the Morgans. The more he thought about it, the angrier he got at Grayson Morgan.

CHAPTER 5

The Great Chamber was hushed as everyone waited for Pan to appear. She had barely been seen since she arrived with Moart'Tor, and neither had he.

Pan entered with Moart'Tor. She led him to the front of the assembly, and while she addressed everyone, had him stand next to her beside the Overseer.

"You have a thousand questions, I am sure. As I do. I see some familiar faces and many unfamiliar ones. In the time I have been gone, much has taken place for all of us. Adults have grown into elders. Offling have grown into adults. New offling have been born. In time, I will learn about those who have returned to the Great Spirit and, with you, grieve their loss.

"As some of you know, this is Moart'Tor. He is my brother's son and was born and raised at the Mothoc rebel camp, which is called Zuenerth. He left Zuenerth for Kayerm, where he met the Sassen and even lived among them for a while. Moart'Tor was raised to believe the Sassen, as well as the Akassa, are an abomination and should be destroyed. He was sent to Kayerm to learn how many of us still lived among them and to bring back information about the Promised One."

Murmurs spread through the crowd.

"No, I have not brought a traitor among you," she continued. "Moart'Tor no longer believes the Akassa and Sassen should be destroyed, but he could not go home to the rebels. They expect him to return with answers, not a testimony, so I have brought him here to live among you. He needs brotherhood, just as each of us does. I ask that you help him fit into Lulnomia and do not judge him for his past misconceptions."

"What of you, Pan? Are you here to stay?" a voice called out.

"How long I stay depends on many factors."

"Where have you been? Where did you go when you left?" another voice asked.

Pan thought the story of Wrollonan'Tor's appearance before the High Council when Hatos'Mok was trying to banish her would have been well known by now; however, she decided it was best not to make assumptions.

"Throughout Mothoc history, we believed there could only be one Guardian of Etera at a time and that the arrival of a second heralded the death of the current Guardian. Wrollonan'Tor was the Guardian prior to my father, and it was said he died, but he did not. He still lives, and in a location inaccessible to most, he has been my teacher and guide for these past thousands of years.

"Through his teaching, I have learned how extensive a Guardian's abilities truly are. Far beyond my father's understanding, to be sure. He has taught me what I need to know, not only better to serve the Great Spirit and Etera but also to train the Promised One when the time comes."

Pan tried not to search the crowd for Rohm'Mok's face but failed. She found him standing in the back to the right with Tala and Vel at his side. Her heart dropped when she saw him and dropped further when she saw Vel next to him. She wanted to leave Lulnomia, but she could not—certainly not until she knew Moart'Tor was going to be fine. How she wished she had not come.

"When will the Promised One come?" one of the Healers asked.

"When he is ready, I will bring him to Lulnomia, but until he achieves full control of his powers, the Promised One will live with Wrollonan'Tor and me."

Moart'Tor asked Pan if he could speak, and she told him to go ahead.

"People of Lulnomia, thank you for opening your arms and hearts to me. I am grateful for your mercy. The Guardian did not tell you, but I went to Kayerm under false pretenses. I went asking for asylum when my true intent was to spy on the Sassen and the Akassa to take information back to the Leader at Zuenerth. But my eyes were opened. Males at Zuenerth are no longer allowed to mate, so females are not allowed to bear offling, and the community is diminishing. The Leader knows their days are numbered, and if he is to carry out his cause, he cannot wait forever. But I pledge my support to the Guardian and to everyone here. I will stand with you against them if it comes to that."

"Thank you, Moart'Tor," Pan said. "We will pray it does not come to that."

She looked the crowd over, seeing the solemn faces and feeling the despondency before she continued. "Hear me, Lulnomia. The Great Heart, the creative substance from which all is formed, and the Great Mind, the unfathomable intellect that effortlessly thinks everything into existence in infinite combinations, complexity, and order, are always working for our benefit. The Order of Functions, under the direction of the Great Will, is still working on behalf of all Etera. Do not lose your faith in these final days. Sooner than you expect, the Promised One will take his place. Hold on to your faith, and do not let your hearts be troubled. Even now, as you feel fear for the future, divine patterns are shifting, forming, and re-aligning to bring about the most beneficial outcome for us all."

She paused. "Go about your lives. Remember that nothing can befall you of which the Great Spirit is unaware. My hope is that one day all the Mothoc will be reunited and that our lost brothers and sisters at Zuenerth will someday take their place with us, as Moart'Tor has."

While the chamber slowly emptied, Pan remained, greeting those who came by to speak with her for a moment. Out of the corner of her eye, she saw her beloved leave with Vel and Tala. Where did they live, she wondered. Irisa said Rohm'Mok had moved out of the Leader's Quarters the day after she left Lulnomia. She wanted to know, and she did not want to know. It was like an open wound that needed time to close but which she could not stop picking at.

When everyone except Irisa had left, Pan said she was retiring to her quarters. She had long ago lost the need to eat, much as Wrollonan'Tor had, but she did sleep as it gave her mind healing time away from the stresses of reality.

As she stood in the open doorway to the Leader's Quarters of the High Rocks community, she took in the dried flowers and herbs and colorful rocks Irisa had earlier brought in to adorn the space, no doubt trying to remove the tomb-like feel that it now had for Pan. She was glad the red jasper had remained undisturbed from its place and went across to admire it.

A voice startled her, and she turned to see Rohm'Mok standing in the doorway. Physically, he had aged some, whereas, being a Guardian with a practically limitless lifespan, she had not. They had both been so young when they were paired, but she found his added maturity made him all the more attractive.

"May I come in?"

"Of course." Pan watched as Rohm'Mok entered and wandered around, looking things over as if remembering.

"I am sure Irisa told you I never came back here once you had left."

"She did. And I understand why."

"I will not keep you long. I only have a few questions. You do not owe me answers, of course, I know that."

"Please—"

"You said you have been with Wrollonan'Tor since you left here. Is this another community nearby?"

"It is only he and I who reside there. Irisa, who, as you know, is his daughter as well as Overseer, comes and goes. It is where she lived through the centuries when she appeared out of nowhere. So, it is not a community as Lulnomia is."

"I see. What is it like?"

"Oh, that is difficult to answer," and Pan chuckled a little in spite of herself. "It is anything you want it to be. It is as real as life here is, but it is just a motion away."

"A motion away? I do not understand."

"Hmmm. Yes, it is difficult. Let us say there is another room of which we are not aware. And that there are people living there whom we cannot see or hear or touch. But their lives are as real to them as ours are here. It is just that, being in another room, they live a little out of sync with our reality."

"So where you live is much like here? With trees and animals and flowers?"

"Yes."

"What did you mean, that it is anything you want it to be?"

"Wrollonan'Tor has taught me so much. I, like him, am able to create the reality I live in. If I wish it to be spring, it is spring. If I long for a day to nurse my sorrows, I can make it rain. If I am lonely or sad, a bear or a fox comes to comfort me. It is a very malleable medium."

"You have sorrows, Pan?"

Hearing him say her name almost broke her. Pan didn't know how to answer, so she waited for Rohm'Mok to continue.

"Wrollonan'Tor. He is your teacher?"

"Teacher, friend, guide, counselor, companion. All of that, to be sure."

"And you have spent these thousands of years learning from him."

"Yes. But, though time passes there as it does here, my experience of it has not been the same as yours. Wrollonan'Tor taught me how to skim through time like a rock skipping over the surface of a lake. The river still flows underneath, but the rock travels far while touching down only at certain points."

Why had Rohm'Mok sought her out? Did he not know how painful it was for her to see him, knowing he was with Vel?

"So you can move forward in time, in a way?" he asked.

"Yes, you can put it like that. Otherwise, the duration would be intolerable."

"Can you also move backward, then?" He paused and met her eyes for the first time. "I am sorry, I did not mean to stay so long. We can talk another time if you wish."

"No, it is alright. Who knows when we will have time again."

Pan suggested he sit and waited while he did so, but she remained standing. Part of her didn't want to have a conversation about such a matter-of-fact topic, but she didn't know what else to talk about, either, so she continued.

"I have realized we move forward on our path according to our will and that the Order of functions constantly adapts to create the best outcome possible. The Great Mind is an unimaginable intellect and can compensate for every act, decision, and change in course. You were going to ask me, if I could go back and change the past, would I? Like everyone else, I have free will. Believe me, I have pondered this question for thousands of years, but I have not been led by the Great Spirit to do any such thing."

"Then it is possible? Would it be allowed?"

"Again, free will. My training has brought me and still brings me into closer and closer alignment with the Great Spirit, which brings my free will closer in alignment, too. If I were ever led to do so, yes, I could go back and change the past, but it can never be for my own personal benefit."

She couldn't stop herself. "What would you have me change?"

"I do not know. Nothing. Or everything, perhaps. Everything that brought us to here." His voice dropped.

Pan did not know what to say, so she continued, "There is no way to avoid sorrow in this life because the Great Spirit gave us free will and that free will acts on the receptive feminine aspect of this world. Our intentions, our active soul movements have an effect on our path. The Order of Functions produces the most beneficial outcome it can, working around the current that our free will, as well as that of others, sets in motion.

"But, tell me, Rohm'Mok, why all the questions?"

"I am stalling. I should just ask you what I came here to ask. Will you be remaining at Lulnomia?"

Pan searched the face she loved for a clue to what he was looking for. They had never had trouble talking to each other in the past, but her actions had changed all of that. "For a while," she answered. "Probably until Moart'Tor adjusts. When the Promised One is ready, I will return with him, but his training will take place as mine did, in Wrollonan'-Tor's realm."

"So you will never live among us again?"

"Rohm, what are you asking me?" Her emotions were about to boil over.

"When you left, I did not think I would survive, but I had to, for Tala's sake. No matter how much I wanted to curl up and die, I had to be strong for her."

"She has turned out to be a fine female, from what I can tell. You and Vel did a wonderful job raising her."

"It was what you asked me to do, to find someone to be a mother to her, and I did. Pan, I need to know if you are returning to your life here or not. Because I cannot go through it again."

"What do you mean?"

"You leaving again. I know a great deal of time has passed, and things are not the same for either of us. But I deserve at least to know what your plans are."

"There are too many unknowns, and one of them is Moart'Tor and his adapting. The Promised One has been born, and I will return with him in only a few years."

"So you *will* be leaving again."

"Yes, but only long enough to go to Kthama and bring back the Promised One. He must be brought here under the protection of Lulnomia, where Wrollonan'Tor and I will help him develop his abilities to the fullest."

Just then, Tala peeked her head into the Leader's Quarters and said, "Father, are you in here? Mother—I mean, Vel—sent me looking for you; she needs your help, and Irisa said I would find you here—"

Pan's heart dropped at hearing Tala refer to Vel as *Mother*. She could also see how uncomfortable Tala was, and her heart went out to her daughter, so she said to Rohm'Mok, "You need to go. Perhaps we will talk another time."

He turned back to face Pan. "Yes, of course. I shouldn't have gotten into all of that. I should only have said, welcome home, Pan."

Irisa stood next to her father.

"How strong she is," Wrollonan'Tor said. "And how happy I am that she returned before Rohm'Mok passed on. For good or bad, they needed to see each other again at least once more." He fell silent, lost in his own thoughts.

Irisa did something she seldom did. She walked over and laid her head on her father's arm, and wrapped her arms around him as far as she could reach. In the centuries that had passed, Irisa had long ago learned that her father avoided physical contact because, in his loneliness, he found avoiding it was the only way not to awaken his deep longing for it.

"Oh, Father, why are you so sad? Are you not happy for Pan that her beloved still lives?"

"Yes, he still lives. I am sad because I know too well what awaits Pan now that she has returned to Lulnomia—to watch those she loves age, wither away, and die. I have been blessed that you have lived so long, Irisa. But in time, you will also leave me. People wish to live forever, but they have no idea of the reality of such an existence."

CHAPTER 6

It was time. Adia, Nootau, and Iella were traveling to the High Rocks. Adia was glad that Eyota and Tansy were going too. Harak'Sar had arranged for several others to help them on their journey, and after a few days, they arrived at Kthama.

So many were gathered together awaiting their return, anxious to greet them. Adia caught sight of Acaraho, and he threw ceremony aside, clasping her in his arms and drawing her up hard against him. She nestled her head under his chin.

"Saraste', I have missed you so," her mate said. "My heart is at peace now that we are all reunited at last."

From Iella's arms, An'Kru reached out to his father. Acaraho propped the offling against his shoulder and turned to the twins, cradled by Nootau.

Oh'Dar, Nadiwani, High Protector Awan, First

Guard Thetis, and Mapiya were all there. Adia hugged everyone, and they welcomed her new offspring back home.

"Where are Acise and I'Layah?" Adia eventually asked.

"They are with my grandmother and Ben. They did not want to overwhelm you. I am sure they are anxious to welcome you home when you have time to visit with them."

"I know it has not been that long, but it seems like an eternity. Oh, to be at rest tonight in our quarters, to walk the familiar halls of Kthama, and to gaze again upon the faces of my loved ones," Adia said, her heart drinking in Oh'Dar's handsome face and startling blue eyes.

"I have much to tell you," Acaraho said, "as I am sure you do too."

"And I want to hear it all. Amazing events have taken place, everything is changing, and I do not see an end in sight for some time."

As they made their way through Kthama, so many others welcomed her home. Adia kept searching the faces, looking for Nimida, but she was not there. And despite her happiness at returning home, the deep sadness over her estranged daughter still remained.

At the evening meal, Ben, Miss Vivian, and several others gathered at the Leader's table with Acaraho and Adia, Ned, Oh'Dar and Acise, Nootau and Iella. The conversation turned to Ned's plans.

"Before I start traveling to the Brothers' village," said Ned, "in order to feel completely comfortable teaching, I want to become more comfortable with the Brothers' language, and there is more I need to learn about their ways. Chief Kotori offered the help of one of his people, so perhaps I would be welcome back at his village to further my learning."

"I agree," Oh'Dar chimed in. "Chief Is'Taqa's village is closer, but you already have established friendships at Chief Kotori's."

"I am not sure I can find my way back, though."

Oh'Dar sighed. Another trip? He had just gotten back from visiting the Governor. "I will take you whenever you are ready." He saw the sympathetic look on his mate's face.

"When you are ready to come back," Miss Vivian offered, "I will be glad to share my experience of teaching English. I am not an expert, but the People seem to be learning it fairly quickly, so I must be doing something right!" She smiled.

Oh'Dar stopped and took a proper look at his grandmother and Ben. It was obvious they were up in years. A painful thought had been nagging him for some time. How long would they be with him? He couldn't bear the thought of losing them, and in addition, their love would be a blessing for I'Layah as she grew.

"I have been thinking, son," Ben said. "What do you think about I'Layah learning about the Waschini world as she grows?"

Acise asked, "What do you mean?"

"I am not suggesting she would leave here to live among our kind, but I think it might help her at least to know about it. Maybe even occasionally visit the Webbs with her father?"

Oh'Dar looked at his life-walker, trying to read her. "I imagine she would be curious about it, just as I was."

"It is part of her heritage," Acise said. "I do not have any real grounds to object. I would just worry about her being out of my sight. She would blend in; that is not a problem, and she will be able to speak fluent English. I just need to get used to the idea; she is still so young."

Further down the table, Nootau could see there was something on his mate's mind. She was fidgeting in her seat. Finally, she addressed Adia. "I would like your permission to take An'Kru into the forest. Oh, I mean, not without you, but I would like to see how he interacts with the birds and animals over a slightly longer period."

"I do not mind. I would also be interested in that.

I do wonder if that will change as he grows and develops language. I mean, when he can form words, will he be able to command them as you do?"

"Remember, I do not command them, I ask them to do things for me, and they willingly comply; I do not have any power over them. I assume it would be the same for him, and I am very curious as we seem to share this same ability."

"Soon then, when it is a little warmer out," Adia added.

It had not even been one day, and Nootau was already concerned about his mate missing her home and her parents. He understood anew what it might have been like for Oh'Dar, feeling the pull to be in more than one place at once.

Nootau could also see the sadness hanging over his mother. He assumed it was still about An'Kru being taken away by Pan in the future, but he also suspected it had to do with Nimida. He had been looking for her since they arrived, with no success, but the High Rocks was a big place, and it was not unusual he might not come across her.

He glanced across the chamber. At another table, Nadiwani and High Protector Awan were having a private meal, seemingly oblivious to the conversation around them.

Later the next morning, Adia was ready to face the truth about whether Nimida and Tar had stayed or had indeed left. Having decided it, Mapiya was the first person she ran into who would know.

Adia broached the subject. "I have not seen Nimida or Tar since I returned."

"Oh, well, I just saw Nimida a moment ago," Mapiya said. "She is repairing some tools."

Adia's heart was pounding as she approached Nimida's workshop. She could hear the scrape and chip-chip of the stones but no voices, so she assumed Nimida was alone.

She clacked the announcement stone and called Nimida's name. "It is Adia; may I come in?"

Nimida came to the door and looked into her mother's eyes. "Yes, of course."

Adia walked in, stepping gingerly around the tool area, "You are still here."

"Yes. The last time we spoke, I admitted that running away would not solve anything and that my problems would go with me, and then I realized how much I would be losing by leaving. So, yes, I am staying. Are you back for good?"

"Yes. The danger has passed, and we were allowed to come home."

"I see." Nimida invited Adia to sit.

"Is there— Is there anything I can do to help you?" Adia asked as she found an available boulder.

"I am glad you came. I would have sought you out before long if you had not. Since we last talked, I have done a lot of thinking about everything you said, about the situation you were in. And as the initial rush of emotions subsided, I was able to look at it more dispassionately and think about what I would have done in your situation. And I have to admit, Adia, I am not sure I could have found a solution that you did not."

Adia folded her hands in her lap and tried to appear calm.

"And, I think I might like to see the twins. Maybe, even look after them sometimes—if you need the help, that is. And An'Kru, of course."

Adia's heart leaped. Was this possible? Was it possible she had not lost her daughter after all? "I would welcome your help, and I would be very happy for you to get to know them."

"But," Nimida said, "someday, I want to know who my father is."

Then, before Adia could speak, she added, "Not yet. I want first to find out who I am now. How I relate to you now. I am not ready to add another complication into the mix." She rearranged the tools at her side.

"If that is best for you, then, yes, of course."

"Does he know?" Nimida looked up and stared right into Adia's eyes.

"Yes. He knows he seeded you—and Nootau.

"We will move at your pace," Adia assured her daughter. "You just tell me when you are ready to visit, whether it is with me or your siblings."

"I will, I promise."

Adia left with a much lighter heart. Nimida had not gone, and they had been able to talk without an emotional flood of pain blocking the possibility of good will between them. She gave thanks to the Great Mother for whatever had helped to ease Nimida's pain and that there was the promise of a relationship between them. Now, if only she could shake her constant dread about An'Kru's future.

Ned and Oh'Dar were ready to return to Chief Kotori's village. They traveled first to Chief Is'Taqa's village to pick up the horses, where Storm whinnied and pawed the ground at seeing his master again.

Oh'Dar met with Chief Is'Taqa and Honovi to discuss what had taken place during his visit with the Governor.

Is'Taqa nodded gravely. "It is as the Guardian Pan said; we must prepare ourselves for what is coming. Though our people here will hopefully be protected by the Waschini laws, that protection does not extend past the villages on the Morgan Trust property."

Oh'Dar did not say it out loud, but he was thinking of Riggs and wondering how much further the constable would take it. He had no doubts that the Governor had dealt with the man and no doubt harshly. Whether that would convince Riggs to drop his vendetta, he could not know, but he did know it could go either way and might simply serve to inflame the constable further.

Oh'Dar and Ned set out, and within a few days, were at Chief Kotori's village. This time, Pakwa was not the first to greet them, and Oh'Dar missed seeing him at his usual fishing spot. Instead, Kele came running toward them as they approached the village perimeter.

He merrily shouted, "Oh'Dar! Ned Webb!"

Ned reached down and hoisted Kele up on his horse, placing him in front, and they rode the short remaining distance into the village.

Immediately, Tiponi came over to welcome them, and then others arrived, including Sakinay, who Ned couldn't help thinking of as Sour Face.

"The Chief is in his shelter; I will tell him of your arrival," Sakinay said.

Oh'Dar and Ned dismounted, and after greeting everyone, took care of their horses.

A little while later, Sakinay found them. "The Chief is meeting with the Elders."

"Ned will be staying with you now for some time, as the Chief agreed to at the last brotherhood meeting," explained Oh'Dar. He realized he had changed the name of the High Council meetings, but it felt somehow appropriate.

Tiponi spoke. "We were prepared for your return. The Chief has said you are welcome for as long as you wish to stay. Your teacher here will be Awantia, who will teach you more of our language and will also be the first to learn Whitespeak."

Ned thanked her, and he and Oh'Dar went off to take care of the horses.

Kele soon arrived with Awantia and Myrica in tow. Awantia laughed, "Alright, Kele, you can let go now. What is so important?"

"Oh'Dar and Ned Webb have returned," Tiponi told the women. "They are caring for their horses."

"Ah," Myrica said. "Now your work begins, Awantia."

"Begins again, you mean. I do not mind," Awantia smiled. "He learned fairly quickly—once Sakinay finished making it hard on him."

As soon as they were out of earshot, Myrica teased her friend, "Your Waschini husband has returned!"

Awantia leaned down, plucked up a handful of grass, and threw it at Myrica. It fluttered harmlessly to the ground without reaching her.

As they put their things in the shelter, Ned said, "With their greater strength, the Sassen rebuilt the village even better than before."

"Yes. I've never seen any shelters so solidly built. I will be leaving in the morning; will you be alright?"

"I'll be fine. These people here, they feel like family to me, now."

"As it should be."

The next day, Ned was besieged with welcomes and smiles, and he returned each one with equal enthusiasm.

As part of his ongoing contribution to the village, he took over the role of helping Myrica and Awantia fill their cookpots. It raised some eyebrows and stirred talk, some of which eventually made it to Sakinay.

One afternoon, Ned saw Sakinay watching him from a short distance away, where he was squatting with his hands dangling between his knees but with his fists balled and his brow furrowed. Ned looked at him a moment and then looked away.

Neither of the two women had noticed it, but Kele, who was never far from Ned, had. "Sakinay does not like you now," the boy said.

"What have I done wrong?"

"You keep the company of these women. He said perhaps the Waschini men have a rutting season like the animals."

Ned was shocked at being compared to female animals in heat but knew Kele was just repeating something he had heard and didn't understand the insulting crassness of Sakinay's remark. It had not occurred to Ned that Sakinay, or anyone else, might misjudge his attentions to Myrica and Awantia, and he looked over at the brave, who had likely heard Kele from that distance.

Sakinay rose, stared at Ned a moment longer, then turned and disappeared into the woods. Apparently, things were not as good between him and Sakinay as he had thought.

CHAPTER 7

Moart'Tor was very popular at Lulnomia. After thousands of years together, the community members were familiar with each other. To have a stranger appear was a novelty and a curiosity. Many of the single females were particularly interested in him because of his striking appearance and relationship to the Guardian.

Irisa, in her position as Overseer, asked that he come and see her. "You have noticed no doubt that many of the females here are taking an interest in you," she said.

"I have," Moart'Tor replied.

. . .

"You are part of Lulnomia now, and in time, you may wish to pair with someone here. It will provide you all the pleasure of companionship and help you become more settled here with us.

Would you be interested in formally being introduced to some of the females?"

"That sounds fine; thank you."

Moart'Tor should have been happier at this news. The idea of having a female at his side had always been a comforting thought, not to mention the physical pleasures it would provide. It had been a common topic of conversation at Zuenerth, where Kaisak had not let anyone pair for some time. Females had to be earned and had he returned home with the information Kaisak wanted, Moart'Tor would have been given a female of his own.

"This does meet with your approval, does it not?" Irisa asked, seeing Moart'Tor's lackluster reaction to what should have been pleasant news.

"Yes. Thank you."

. . .

"Perhaps I am being insensitive. Did you leave someone behind? Someone for whom you are missing?" she asked, leaning forward a little.

"No, I was never paired. Nor was there any special female. Since I knew there was only a remote chance of being paired, I did not let myself entertain the idea of anyone in particular."

"Then I will move ahead. If you trust my judgment, it will help quell the spread of disappointment to narrow the pool of females. I will make arrangements for you to meet them once the research is done."

"Thank you, Overseer," he said. He rose to leave, perplexed at his own reaction.

Later Irisa spoke with Pan, "He did not seem very happy about it. You do not think he is thinking of leaving, do you?"

"I sense none of that in him," Pan said.

. . .

"Neither do I. But there is a sadness there."

"I can also feel that. I had thought it was homesickness from not being able to return to Zuenerth, but other than missing his mother and brothers and being worried for their futures there, that is not it, I can tell. He seems to have no longing to return there."

"And that should not quell his interest in pairing," Irisa remarked. "I do find him to be truthful."

"He will not betray us. He wants to be here, for the most part."

Pan and Irisa were both right. Moart'Tor did want to be at Lulnomia. To find another community of his own kind—and an expansive community at that—was a blessing beyond his imaginings. The extensive structure of Lulnomia comforted him, and the contented mood of the community was in sharp contrast to the anger and despair back home. He wished all of Zuenerth could learn what he had learned and would realize the Akassa and Sassen were not abominations needing to be destroyed. He imagined the life they could all have here if they would stop believing Kaisak's lies and abandon his misguided cause.

He wondered if Kayerm was now empty once more. That made him sad to think about. At times, he had been happy there, even though he was not one of them. He had known moments of peace, more so than in all the centuries growing up among his own kind. He never did learn where the Sassen were living. How many more were there? And what of Eitel and her brother?

That was it. He realized it just then. He missed Eitel. Generous, sweet, and beautiful Eitel, the kindness in her eyes when she looked at him, that gentle touch when she had tried to console him. How he regretted pulling away from that touch. With her glistening pitch-black hair and her eyes that were nearly black, she was beautiful inside and out. So that was what was troubling him. Oh, but it was hopeless, he lived at Lulnomia now, and there was no going back. Somehow he had to forget her and move forward. But try as he might, he could not rid his mind of the image of her at his side or in his arms. Perhaps pairing would help him move forward and allow his memories of Eitel to fade away.

Weeks passed, and Pan kept herself busy while keeping an eye out for Rohm'Mok and Vel. She avoided them, not wanting to face the painful truth of their relationship. At night she returned, alone, to the Kthama Leader's Quarters. She tossed and turned, unable to make peace with the memories. Finally, she approached Irisa about it.

"I do not wish to stay in the Leader's Quarters."

"Too many memories?" Irisa asked, searching Pan's eyes.

"Yes, and I am not Kthama's Leader; Vel is. Why did she not move into the Leader's Quarters with Rohm'Mok and Tala?

"That is a conversation you need to have with her—or them. And she only accepted temporary leadership of Kthama," Irisa reminded her.

. . .

"With no idea of when I might return, that was a liberal use of the term temporary."

"Still, it was her choice."

"I cannot stay with your father as I did before; I need to be here to ensure Moart'Tor is adjusting," Pan said. "There must be other quarters I can use; there used to be many available living spaces."

"Our population has grown, as you can see. But there are; I will find you another place," Irisa said softly.

"Thank you."

Later that evening, Pan returned to the Leader's Quarters, intending to turn in early. Her heart was filled with unrest. She was home, but it did not feel like home. It was empty and lonely, and what had been happy memories of her and her mate and daughter were too painful to consider.

A voice behind her made her turn.

. . .

It was Rohm'Mok. "I am sorry; I did not mean to startle you. It seems I did this to you once before."

"I was not expecting company, and you did not announce—"

"I apologize; the door was open," he said as his eyes swept the room.

"Forgive my abruptness, but what is it you want?" Pan felt her voice catch.

"You have been avoiding me, it seems," he said, running his hand over the surface of the stone table where they had shared meals so very many years ago.

"I have been very busy."

"Of course. Still—"

Pan thought she was going to lose control. Why was he there? Did he not know how much it hurt to see him? Was he punishing her for leaving, or was it possible he had no idea how much she still loved him? She watched him walk about the room as he had last time, looking at first this area, then the next, as if replaying the past in his mind. He stopped in front of the 'Tor Leader's Staff, stored securely in its corner.

"Is there something you wanted to talk about?" she finally said.

"So many memories. That is why I never came back here after you left."

"Rohm'Mok, *please*. If you have a point, please make it—"

"You did not answer me. I asked you earlier, here, in this room, before Tala entered and interrupted us. And I have been waiting all this time for you to tell me."

"Tell you what?"

. . .

"Are you staying here or not? Pan, I need to know; I think I have a right to know."

"I did answer you. I said I would be here for a while. And that in time, I will have to leave and will return again with the Promised One. He must be kept safe, and only here at Lulnomia can his expanding powers be shielded from the rebels' knowledge."

Why are you here, Rohm? What did he want her to say?

"This was our home. We were happy here once—" his voice trailed off.

"Once, a long time ago. And then everything changed," she said quietly.

"Not everything," he said.

"Everything that mattered," Pan's voice broke. "Everything that mattered to me. I lost you. I lost Tala. She does not even remember me, does she?"

. . .

"She was very young when you left."

"It seems you will not rest until you have a definitive answer from me about how long I will be staying. I am sorry, I cannot give you that."

Rohm'Mok walked slowly toward her.

Pan's eyes widened, and when he was close, she put her hands up and backed away. "Stop. What are you doing? You are with Vel. Irisa told me that together you and Vel have led Kthama."

"Yes, Vel and I have ruled Kthama together. Vel has been a friend, a confidant, an advisor, and a mother to Tala. She has shared my troubles and helped me bear my burdens. She has been at my side whenever I needed her. But never in my bed. And never in my heart."

Rohm'Mok closed the distance between them, took Pan's hand, and looked deeply into her eyes. "I told you before, long ago, and the thousands of years have not changed it. There will never be another for me, no matter what you say. And just as the choice of

Bak'tah-Awhidi was not up to me, whether I ever let another into my heart was not up to you."

Tears silently rolled down Pan's cheeks. "You waited? Never knowing if I would return in your lifetime? You waited for me." She fell into the arms of her beloved.

Rohm'Mok wrapped his arms around her, as he had longed to do for thousands of years. He whispered into her ear, "There was no other choice. I told you. There is no one but you for me, and there never will be. I am here if you will have me again."

Then he leaned back to meet her eyes. "Unless, unless there is another in your heart now. Wrollo-nan'Tor?"

"No! Oh no, only you, my love. Only and always you." Rohm'Mok leaned back in and pressed his lips to Pan's. She yielded her body to his, and the warmth and comfort of his embrace surrounded her once more. She sobbed with happiness. "Oh, my love. I cannot believe you waited for me. It is more than anyone deserves."

. . .

"Shhh. Do not cry, Saraste'. You are home again. Home again, and back in my arms where you belong."

When they disengaged, his eyes searched hers for the answer to the question he wanted to ask next. And she answered him by kissing him again, this time long and deep. Then she moved across the room and closed the stone door, blocking out the rest of the world.

He took her gently at first, then greedily, showing her how much he missed her and needed her, and she met his passion with her own. They were locked together as they had been before, sharing their devotion and need and longing for each other. For a while, all the troubles of their lives, the pain, and the disappointments were gone, and there was only joy and gratitude and peace in their hearts.

CHAPTER 8

The next morning, Pan awoke with Rohm'Mok beside her, and her heart leaped all over again. She turned over and watched him sleep, as she had so long ago. She counted his breaths as his chest rose and fell. She studied every line of his face, now older but still so handsome. Her mind began to wander to the lost years, but she stopped herself. They were together again, and that was what mattered. There was no wisdom in lamenting the mistakes of the past.

Were they mistakes? No. She knew in her heart and soul that she had done what was given to her to do in the service of the Great Spirit. She had never been more certain of anything in her lifetime. Of course, that it had caused heartache for her and her loved ones grieved her spirit, but it did not mean she had chosen wrongly. And in time, it would all be worked out. The Promised One would take his place, and Etera would be restored to her original perfection. She knew that the six years left before she returned with An'Kru would pass, oh, so quickly, and then his training would begin. In the meantime, she still had the six male Sassen Guardians to teach.

Her thoughts wandered to Vel, who, long ago, before they left for Lulnomia, had asked at the Kthama High Council to be paired. And now, thousands of years had passed, and she was still alone. Or was she? It occurred to Pan that perhaps Vel had paired after all and that the idea she had not was an assumption.

Rohm'Mok stirred beside her, opened his eyes, and smiled. He raised a hand to gently caress Pan's face. "Saraste'."

Then he sat up. "So, do you still want to move to other quarters?"

"How do you know about that?"

"Irisa told me, and she said that you thought Vel and I were together. Looking back, I can see how you would have thought that, so I knew it was time I settled it clearly, time to face my fears and find out if you would still have me."

"Yes, a thousand times, yes."

"So shall I move in here with you?" His eyes never left hers.

"Yes. Let us start anew. But what of Tala? Does she not live with you—wherever that is?"

"Tala lives with her best friend. They share a

living space and seem to enjoy each other's company."

"So, where do you live, if not with Tala, or as I have learned, not with Vel?"

"After you left, I was lost. For a very long time, I was angry with the Great Spirit for asking this of you. You had already suffered so much in your life. Losing your father to the vortex, then Dak'Tor's betrayal and theft of the crystal. And I was angry that Tala had lost her mother, and I had lost my true love. Though I have to say it was just as well you left while Tala was so young. In time, she bonded with Vel. The only female who could have loved her more than Vel did would be you."

"I owe Vel so much."

"She knows. We talked so often about you, about how much we both missed you. After you left, she put the Leader's Staff back in its place, though she had to do it alone. In all that time, I never stepped foot in here again. It was too painful. Irisa explained where you had gone, so I knew she had knowledge of you, but I never asked because I could not bear to know. I hope you understand."

"I do. Wrollonan'Tor has taught me so much. My abilities are so much more advanced than I could have imagined they would be. I had the power to see what your life was like and what was going on here, but I refused to use it. The risk of further heartbreak was so great that I could not. It was the same with Dak'Tor. I knew he was alive and not suffering and that wherever his path had led him was for his benefit, so I never visited him—and the rebel camp—either."

"Visited?" he asked.

"In a way. It is a way of overseeing what is going on without being seen by those who are there."

"That is astounding. Tala and I moved into other quarters here in the High Rocks section. Most days while she was growing up, she spent time with Vel or Inrion."

Rohm'Mok and Pan lay in each other's arms for some time. He told her about the others there who Pan knew so well and what had happened to them over the years. She told him about some of the abilities Wrollonan'Tor had taught her and of the deep friendship that had developed between the three of them, her, Wrollonan'Tor, and Irisa. She was grieved to hear that Trac had returned to the Great Spirit, which explained why she had not seen him with Toniss.

"How is Toniss, though?" she asked. "I am sure she is lonely without Trac."

"She misses Trac, of course. But she does have great-grandlings to care for."

"Grandlings?" Pan laughed.

"I think it is something Tala made up; she is very creative. Oh, and we now have newlings—the tiny offling when they are first born."

"I want to spend time with her, get to know her."

"She wants that too."

Pan squeezed her eyes shut, hard.

"Do not be sad, my love. We must make the best of what we have. But if I could turn back time, if I could arrange it so you never had to make such a terrible sacrifice, I would."

"It had to be. If there could have been another way, the Order of Functions would have laid that path before me," Pan said.

Pan rested her head on his chest. She breathed in his warm male scent, which she had missed for so long. She could hear his strong heartbeat, and each beat represented now, this moment—that this time was not lost to her. She must not squander it with regrets about the past and what might have been. She was reunited with her beloved, and it was not given to all females to raise offling. She must be grateful that her daughter was alive, healthy, and happy and that she knew love and tenderness and was not burdened with inconsolable grief over the loss of a mother she had built years of memories with. For Tala, it had indeed been kinder this way. Not perfect, but perhaps the best it could be, considering the circumstances.

Someone clacked the announcement stone against the outside of the door. Pan called out, "Who is it?"

It was Irisa. "I have brought you something to eat."

Rohm'Mok rose and opened the stone door. Irisa stood holding out a bowl filled generously with various greens, roots, and meat. "Pan, I am sorry there are no longfish this morning; I know it is your favorite."

She handed Rohm'Mok the large bowl, and he thanked her. Irisa smiled at them both before leaving.

"How did she know?" Rohm'Mok asked.

"I am not sure. In all this time, I still have not entirely figured her out. But she has Guardian blood in her, which may account for her longevity, and, I suppose, the other mysteries about her.

Irisa was happy for Pan and Rohm'Mok. She was grateful that Pan had returned while Rohm'Mok was not only still alive but also young enough for them still to have centuries together. But her heart was also sad, remembering her father's words about how the life of a Guardian was one of service and heartbreak. In time, Pan, too, would lose everyone she loved.

Irisa had lived far longer than any Mothoc could expect to, and she knew she was nearing the end of her life span. The Great Spirit had told her, one day when she was deep in prayer, that she would live to see the Promised One but had shown her nothing beyond that. And after she returned to the Great Spirit, would Pan's friendship and companionship be enough for Wrollonan'Tor? Eventually, while he lived, the only constant in each other's lives would be each other.

Before long, Pan sought out her eldest sister and explained why she had kept her distance, that she had not been ready to face the idea that Vel and Rohm'Mok were paired. The reunion was a happy one, and they spent hours together talking about Tala.

"I do not know how to build a relationship with her," Pan confided in her sister. "She is no longer the young offling I abandoned, and now we are strangers to each other."

"I assure you, sister," Vel consoled her, "in no way does Tala believe you abandoned her or that you abandoned her father, or Inrion or me—or any of Lulnomia. She understands responsibility, and she understands that you were fulfilling your duty to the Great Spirit. You will see, in time, as you get to know her."

"Rohm'Mok told me she lives with a friend. Neither of them ever paired? In all this time?"

"Look at me; in all this time I have not paired either. Some pair late. Some never at all. Either may turn out to be the case for Tala and her friend," Vel suggested.

"There is something I want to ask," she continued. "Now that you are back, will you assume leadership of the High Rocks?"

Pan pondered the question a moment. "No. I am back, but I will still need to live in two worlds—this one and the one with Wrollonan'Tor. It is best that you continue to lead Kthama."

"Rohm'Mok has prepared Tala well, and she is ready to take over leadership if it is needed. Once you spend some time with her, I believe you will agree."

Morvar'Nul, Nofire'Nul, and Vollen'Nul were clearly agitated. "Why does Father not allow one of us to find Moart'Tor?" Nofire asked, tossing some more logs on the morning fire.

"I do not know, brother," Vollen, the youngest of Kaisak's sons, answered.

"I would go, but he says no, that we must wait for his return," Morvar lamented. "Mother is also upset with him. We can all hear them arguing even from the center of the village."

"Useaves says nothing about it. It is hard to tell what that old female is thinking—if she can even think, as old as she is!" Vollen added. He rotated the stick with part of his breakfast skewed on it, savoring the smell of cooking rabbit. It would take more than one rabbit to make a meal, but it was enough to get his morning started.

"She has gotten less vocal lately, but I wonder if she has some magic formula keeping her alive," Nofire commented.

"Now that Dak'Tor's mate, Iria, is the Healer, it seems Useaves does nothing any more but sit around the fire, even in the heat of summer. I do not know how she bears it," Vollen said.

Morvar finished skewering his meat. "It seems the elderly are often cold, so maybe it is her time. Or it is nearing."

"Perhaps if I did go and find Moart'Tor, Father would let me have a female," he continued. "He promised one to Moart'Tor when he returned, so I think it would also apply to me."

"I know who you would pick, too!" Vollen teased his brother. "Nakai!"

"The most beautiful female here? I wish you luck with that!" Nofire said. "And one of Dak'Tor's daughters at that."

"What difference does that make?" Morvar returned. "Dak'Tor sired Moart'Tor, but not any of us."

"It is not the blood that is the issue; it is her. She is feisty. And also, Dak'Tor is protective of his daughters."

"I can handle her; I have watched our father handle Mother all my life!"

"What about Lurir? She is equally beautiful," Nofire said.

"No, not her. Her piercing grey eyes are too much

like a Guardian's. I would fear she might have secret abilities, like perhaps knowing what I was thinking before I did," Morvar said.

Just then, their mother, Visha, came over and stood, hands on her hips. "What are you all doing sitting around talking this morning? Did you just put more wood on the fire? Stop wasting it if you have already eaten! Morvar, you are too old to be sitting around like this. You should already be out hunting for evening meal. And you too, Nofire. Vollen is the only one young enough to be acting so irresponsibly."

"It is still early, Mother. I will get to it, I promise," Morvar reassured her. "We were just talking about Moart'Tor."

Visha looked off into the distance and shook her head. "He has been gone long enough, but we must wait and hope for the best."

"I could go and look for him," Morvar said.

"No," Visha answered. "Your father must have his reasons for not sending someone after your brother, though I do not understand them. I just pray Moart'Tor is alive and well and will return soon because I am sick of fighting about it."

"Everyone hears you," said Vollen.

"I know; it is not good for our community that we argue so. It only creates dissension, and we are already all stressed enough."

"I think we should just go there and kill the Akassa," Nofire stated. "Father has waited too long. Soon the oldest among us will be useless as fighters if they are not already. Our strength is waning."

"No, we have no idea of their numbers, and we do not know where Kthama even is," Morvar corrected his younger brother. "The best we could do would be to find Kayerm, and that means taking on the Sassen and the other Mothoc. It would be hard enough taking on the Akassa and the Mothoc at Kthama, but the Elders have said the Sassen are built like us, only a bit smaller. It would be foolhardy to go into battle with no idea of what we are facing."

"If the Sassen are not that much smaller than we are, what of their females?" Nofire asked. "Maybe we could—"

Morvar thought a moment. "That is a very good question, brother." He felt a quickening in his loins as he imagined it. An entire flock of Sassen females?

"Surely you are joking!" Vollen exclaimed, jumping up from where he was sitting. "You would mate with an abomination? What do you think the Great Spirit would think of that?!"

"Oh, settle down, brother; I was just joking," Morvar said. Only he wasn't. Now that the idea had been planted in his mind, he would be giving it some serious thought. "Besides, how do you know the Great Spirit would frown on that? It would be a way to keep the Mothoc blood flowing on Etera. I am not talking about pairing with them, just using them for offling."

Nofire calmed down, "When you put it like that, well, perhaps. But not to be treated as our equals."

"Of course not. And when they were past bearing age, they could be dispensed with or kept to serve us. Whatever is most beneficial."

Visha listened to her sons' conversation, "I am not sure how I feel about what you are proposing. It might not be a bad idea. I am going to pick the right time and suggest it to your father. He will reject it outright, I am sure, but perhaps, over time, he might warm to the idea. You may be on to a solution, son. Now please, get to your work, or your father will be angry."

Visha walked away, mulling over Nofire's idea. Why couldn't the Mothoc mate with the Sassen? It would depend on the size difference, to be sure. There was a risk to the mother Sassen, yes, depending on the size of the growing offling inside her. But surely, some of them would survive. They could kill the male offling, and when the females were old enough, breed them, too. The entire point would be that, eventually, the offling would have more and more Mothoc blood in them. Perhaps this was a way to create more breeding possibilities. Yes, she would have to pick her moment carefully to tell Kaisak about this, but the more she considered it, the more she truly thought Nofire was on to something there.

The moment came in their quarters a few nights later after Visha had vigorously mated Kaisak, and he was relaxed and almost in a good mood. As they were lying together, she gingerly broached the subject.

"There might be wisdom in not destroying the Sassen females right away. The males, yes, of course, but what of the females? Could they not be of some use to us?"

"Hmmph. I surely do not see how. Do you mean as slaves? Well, possibly that. They are smaller and so probably could not do much harm to any of us unless they organized a specific attack, but we could keep them separated so they could not plot against us. What made you think of that?"

"It is from a suggestion one of your sons made. Only it was not about using them as work slaves, but more of as breeders."

Kaisak frowned. "Breeders? For our males to mate?"

Visha explained further and waited for his outright rejection of the idea, but when none came, she kept quiet.

"What would be the wise thing to do, I wonder," he thought out loud. "I have always considered them an abomination to be destroyed, but if we could breed them until the offling had mostly Mothoc blood running in their veins, killing the females might be considered wasteful in the eyes of the Great Spirit."

"It was Nofire's idea," she volunteered, knowing that he was Kaisak's favorite. He never challenged his father the way the others did. "It was an offhand comment, really, but you may decide it has merit. With each generation, more and more of our blood would enter Etera." Visha stroked his hair, trying to keep him relaxed and in a good mood.

"I believe it could be done. They are not that much smaller than we are. And we could also just pick the largest of the females. But would our males accept this idea?"

"I believe so, in time, if you start changing their opinions, which are based on yours. Their loins are burning. Of course, there might be dissension among the females."

"Perhaps we could keep some of the males to breed with the females," Kaisak mused out loud.

He sat up, and Visha stopped petting him.

"I think Nofire has come up with an innovative solution," he continued. "The only problem is that we would have to defeat all the Mothoc and the male Sassen at Kayerm to get the females. Not knowing how many there are has stopped me from sending our warriors in before now."

"Give the idea time to ferment. Perhaps the solution will come later." To seal his good mood, Visha set to arousing and satisfying Kaisak again, making this night memorable in many ways in hopes of positively rooting the idea in his mind.

Iria had become the Healer to the population of Zuenerth. Useaves could feel her time on Etera was almost up, so she had taken a back seat, merely serving as advisor when asked. In a way, she was relieved she would most likely not live to see the Guardian's return with the Promised One—if that was even going to happen. So much time had passed, and they had stopped talking about it.

Useaves realized that Kaisak was a better Leader than Laborn had been. He did not keep everyone at odds with each other, not purposefully. There was tension now, but it was mating tension. Kaisak tried to keep the males loaded with work, to the point of physical exhaustion, in hopes of quelling their growing frustrations at not having access to the females. As for the females, they were also unhappy. Most of them wanted offling to love and care for, a family.

Though she never said it to Kaisak, ironically, he was now in the same position Moc'Tor had been when there were no more safe breeding choices. In addition, it was nearing past time to annihilate the Sassen and the Akassa, even if Kaisak would not admit it. But she kept her opinion to herself nowadays, wanting peace in her waning years.

What increased the frustration of the unpaired males and females was that those already paired continued to reproduce. There was no reason to prevent them from mating, and they were free to enjoy the sounds of their healthy offling playing in the center of the community. Many of the others were consumed with jealousy and resentment. Anarchy was a beat away, and Useaves didn't know how much longer it would be before something bad happened.

Gard approached his mother, huddled in her usual place over a morning fire. She had a bison hide wrapped around her, serving as a tent to trap in the warmth from the fire. Over time he had forgiven her, as she was the only kin he had, but he never trusted her again; he had learned that lesson. He saw her shivering and tossed some more wood into the fire. Embers flew up from around them. "That will help, I hope," he said.

She glanced up, and he saw how tired her eyes looked. They both knew her time was coming to an end.

"What can I do for you today?" He never referred to her as his mother, and even after all this time, it seemed no one knew of their relationship.

"Nothing. I am content to sit here and try to warm my old bones."

Despite her answer, Gard went to find her something for breakfast. She readily took it when he handed it to her.

Iria soon came over, as she did every morning, bringing hot willow bark tea to ease the old Healer's pain. Whatever was wrong was eating her up from within. Useaves had never been overweight, but now she was practically skin and bones. She needed the A'Pozz plant leaves for her pain, but Iria had used up the stores to ease Visha's mother's pain when she accidentally disturbed a nest of venomous snakes.

The A'Pozz only bloomed after the warm weather started, so, unfortunately, Useaves would have to suffer a while longer yet, if she even lived until then.

Iria sat while the ailing female drank the tea, hoping to take Useaves' mind off her discomfort.

"How is Alta's training coming?" Useaves asked in her lackluster voice.

"She is bright and at any time could easily take over for me," Iria answered.

"And Lurir?"

Iria knew that her daughter was of particular interest to Useaves and had been from the time of her birth. Though she bore only a small patch of the silver-white hair, her eyes were as steel grey as a Guardian's. Iria suspected that Useaves was still expecting Lurir'Tor at some point to display some Guardian abilities. "She is learning equally fast. It is good to have more Healers here."

"A risk I refused to take until I had to when I

trained you. Duplication makes one vulnerable to replacement."

"But withholding some key knowledge tends to balance that out," Iria replied. She had still not been given the antidote to Useaves' poison and had come to doubt one even existed.

"In time, Healer. All will be made known in time." Useaves leaned in closer to the fire.

All in all, Dak'Tor and Iria had seven offling. Isan'Tor was their oldest son and had his father's markings. Next was Lurir with the grey Guardian-colored eyes and the silver-white fur on her back. Then came Nakai, who had her mother's luxurious dark coloring. These three were grown adults now, but two sons and two daughters, much younger, still lived with them.

Dak'Tor had seeded many others through the females Laborn had demanded he mount, building the army with which the Leader intended to destroy the Akassa and Sassen. But that initial plan, continued by Kaisak, had landed them up at the same endpoint, with not enough safe combinations to allow additional pairings. In their fervor to produce an army, both Leaders had ignored the advice of the researchers to selectively match male and female bloodlines.

As a result, the future seemed bleak, which added to the community's overall depression. The only ones who seemed oblivious to the sadness were the offling who still ran and played as their parents had once done.

Dak'Tor sought out Iria to see if she needed help with anything.

She had just returned from gathering wood, accompanied by the eldest and youngest of their sons, Isan'Tor and Osa'Tor. Each had a full armful for the evening fire. "We had to travel quite a way this time. Osa accidentally stumbled into a creek and is chilled—he asks if we can start the fire now," she chuckled.

Dak'Tor took Osa's bundle and started working on the fire.

"Where are Lurir and Nakai?" Dak'Tor asked his other son.

It was Isan'Tor's duty to watch out for them as they were of pairing age, and Dak'Tor did not like how some of the young males looked at his grown daughters. Each was particularly beautiful in her own way. The other two were still very young and would be with Iria's parents, who often watched them during the day.

"Lurir'Tor and Nakai are both helping Dazal and Vaha today," Isan'Tor answered.

Dak'Tor felt the tension leave him. He knew they were safe with Dazal, who was his best friend, and Dazal's mate, Vaha, loved them as if they were her own. How he wished he could know they would always be safe. No one had ever taken a female Without Her Consent, but with the mounting tension, he questioned how effective that prohibition still was. His sons knew better than to leer at the females as many of the other young males did, and he wished other fathers had raised their sons with as much self-restraint as he demanded of his own.

Of particular concern was Morvar, Kaisak's eldest son. His second eldest, Dak'Tor corrected himself. In theory, Moart'Tor was the oldest offling in their family, though Dak'Tor, not Kaisak, had seeded him. And Dak'Tor knew in his heart that the distinction mattered to the Leader, no matter how much he tried to hide it. The question was, through the years, had Kaisak been able to hide it more successfully from Visha?

As Dak'Tor was wondering this, Visha was helping her father, Krac. Her mother had recently returned to the Great Spirit after surprising a nest of poisonous snakes. Ordinarily, a snake bite would not kill one of them, but there had been many adults coiled together, and she had lain there undiscovered for some time. Despite Useaves and Iria's best efforts, Kerga had succumbed and died, and Krac had not been the same since. Though the relationship between her father and mother had been heated, he missed her terribly, so Visha spent as much time as she could caring for him. Now she stood over her father, who was seated before her, and kneaded his aching muscles.

"You are a good daughter," Krac said. "So like your mother. You have her fire and strength."

"Father, something is bothering me, and I need someone to talk to. You and mother are the only ones I can trust, and now with her gone—"

Krac sighed as Visha worked the knots out of his shoulders and arms. "Then tell me, what is troubling you?"

"Moart'Tor never returned, and Kaisak refuses to send anyone after him. It has been long enough, and what if Moart'Tor is hurt or is being held against his will?"

"That hulking son of yours? Oh, no, no one would have the strength to imprison him. Not even a hundred Sassen," he exaggerated, "if there even are that many any longer. As for being hurt, Moart'Tor is very resourceful. He would recover from an injury."

"I just wish Kaisak would send someone after him." She kept working a particularly stubborn knot.

"What is his reasoning for not doing so?"

"He says we must be patient. That no doubt Moart'Tor is learning about the Akassa and the Sassen, and if anyone goes after him, it will contradict the story that he sneaked away to find sanctuary at Kayerm."

"I am not sure I follow that reasoning. But, no

matter, what is it that you do not believe?" her father asked. He knew her well.

"I do not see how sending someone else to find him would cause a problem. They could make up a story that they followed him."

"That might have worked shortly after he left here, but by now, any tracks would be gone."

"Well, maybe he slipped up, and he told someone where he was going, and they just now came forward?" Visha was trying everything she could think of.

"Possibly that might work. But you have not answered my question." He rolled his shoulders. "Ahhhhh, that is good, thank you. Now could you work on my left calf?"

Visha knelt at her father's feet. "When we were paired, Kaisak promised to raise Moart'Tor as one of his own and to protect and love him in spite of not having seeded him," she said.

"I remember having a similar conversation with him before he started pursuing you," Krac said.

"For the most part, I believe he did right by Moart'Tor, but now, his reluctance to send someone to find him bothers me, and I cannot let it go."

"Moart'Tor took on a noble mission for our people, to learn about the Akassa and the Sassen and the Mothoc living among them, and perhaps even to learn of the Promised One. If he has failed and his true motive has been discovered, then sending others after him would subject them to whatever Moart'-

Tor's fate was. I know this is hard to hear, but I believe Kaisak is right in his reasoning."

Visha continued to work on her father's leg. If her mother had been there, she would have understood. Something was not right, and Kerga would also have picked up on it.

CHAPTER 9

Riggs took off his leather work gloves and smacked them together to get the sawdust off. Then he took his hat off and beat it against his thigh for the same reason. He had been chopping wood for days, it seemed. That and mucking out the stables. John and Mary's boys pitched in when they got home, but by then, Riggs had most of it done, so they went on to studying and helping their father with smaller tasks.

He stared at the blisters on his palms. It seemed as if they had just cleared up when another set started. He wasn't cut out for this; no way. The only good part of it was that he had lots of time to think—and think he did.

He knew he couldn't stay with his sister and her family forever. In time, he would be expected to move on. But to where? He and his sister had no other living relatives except far out West, and neither was even sure they were still alive. His only other close relative apart from Mary had been their great uncle in Braxton, who had died during the Morgan trial. He also didn't like the thought of starting over somewhere else, not knowing anyone, hunting for work, staying in cheap boarding houses, and doing manual labor all his life. That would break down a man like him quicker than anything. What he needed was a way to make a living that didn't involve physical labor, and if it hadn't been for Grayson Morgan, he would still be the constable, a man of respect and who could even command some level of fear.

The more Riggs blamed Grayson Morgan, the easier it became for him to think that Morgan should be the one to support him. After all, it was Grayson Morgan's fault he was out of work. But how? He couldn't ask him for a job. There was nothing Riggs could do for him, and neither would he want to. Except—

The thought had been rattling around in the back of Riggs' mind for some time. He went over it and over it, looking for flaws or weak links in the plan. He had thought of each contingency and then considered a response. Now, he decided, he had a foolproof way of never having to work another day in his life.

Until recently, Riggs had thought he must find out what was going on up there, on the Morgan Trust property, but he realized he didn't have to find out.

Oh, there had been a time when that was all he wanted, to expose whatever Morgan was doing up there and put a stop to it. That was when he was gainfully employed and enjoyed the status and luxuries few men knew. But it was all different now, and he didn't need to know what was going on up there. Morgan knew, and what mattered was that he didn't want anyone else to know.

He was going to blackmail Grayson Stone Morgan the Third. But, unlike Tucker when he had tried to blackmail Newell Storis, Riggs was going to get away with it.

Confident there were no flaws in his plan, one evening at the dinner table, he said, "I want to thank you, John and Mary, for letting me stay here all this time. I know no one wants a guest for this long. I really appreciate it, but when the weather heats up, I will be moving on."

John was chewing, and Mary was looking at her husband, waiting for him to say something. When he had swallowed, he said, "Are you sure, Samuel? You aren't in the way here, and the boys and I certainly appreciate the work you're doing."

"I'm sure. It's about time I moved on. You fed me and gave me a roof over my head and time to figure out what I was going to do next, and I have. So I'll probably be leaving early in the summer. I just wanted to let you know."

Riggs waited for them to ask what he was going to do, but they said nothing. That meant he didn't have to use the cover story he had cooked up. Just as well; the fewer people who knew of his whereabouts, even a supposed one, the better.

Spring was fully underway, and the People started spending more time outside. It was time to plant and relish the return of the longer days. Though they did not welcome the heat that was not long off, the springtime buoyed up their moods, and the return of the abundant season of provision reminded them of the faithfulness of the Great Spirit.

Iella was well into her apprenticeship. Just as Adia had been with Urilla Wuti, Iella was a quick study and ate up everything Adia covered with her. Though Iella knew some of it already, she appreciated the opportunity to ask Adia about her particular experience with specific ailments, injuries, and troubles. When they did not have a patient to care for, they would sit and go over the uses, storage, and drawbacks of various herbs and flowers. Usually gathered together on the floor between them would be Aponi, Nelairi, and An'Kru.

The twins were enthralled with An'Kru. Though they were so very young, something about him resonated with them deeply. As soon as they saw him, they would turn their heads and stare, smiling or giggling as they did so. An'Kru was just as interested in them, and it warmed both Healers' hearts to watch them bond.

"Is he going to have this effect on every living creature?" Iella mused.

"It seems that is how it will be."

"Remember what we talked about?" Iella said. "About seeing how An'Kru and I interact with Etera's creatures together? The weather is much warmer now, and I thought we might try soon?"

"Of course. It will be interesting. I need to learn as much about him as I can, and I think that because you have what seems like the same ability, it will give us insight in a way not otherwise possible."

They waited for a particularly warm day, and leaving the twins in Mapiya's care, took An'Kru out into the forest. They picked a beautiful spot in a little grove and sat down in the shade of a towering oak, its trunk surrounded by the thick, soft moss of the forest floor.

No sooner had Adia set An'Kru down than a wood chipper poked its head out from around the tree. His little nose twitched up and down, his whiskers moving with it. He flicked his head from side to side, looking around, before scampering over to sit upright in front of An'Kru, who did nothing but stare at the little creature before him. Then, out crept a rabbit. It, too, sniffed the air and then quietly hopped closer to An'Kru. Overhead, a brown bird alighted and peered down at them, cocking its head from side to side.

Both Healers watched in silence. Finally, not sure if her voice would scare them away, Iella spoke as softly as possible.

"Here is the first thing I noticed," she whispered. "I have to intentionally call them to me; I have to enter a quiet place deep within myself and make the request. Yet with him, there seems to be nothing like that; they are simply drawn to him of their own free will. They are not responding to any call of his own."

"That is interesting. I believe you are right. He did not seem to be trying to get them to come. But of course, who knows? Can an offspring this young form an intention? Or is it, as you suspect, just his nature that calls them to him?"

Adia looked around as best she could without moving too much. She could see other creatures approaching; first, a squirrel perched on the same limb next to the little brown bird, then a fox slowly drew closer. Adia glanced at Iella and raised her eyebrows. What would happen when the fox came into the fold? Surely the rabbit would recognize it as a predator? She felt disappointed, thinking this would break up the little circle that surrounded her son.

Oddly enough, the rabbit did not run off. Not even when the fox sauntered forward and stood next to it, thick red tail flicking back and forth.

"This should not be happening," Iella whispered in disbelief. "I would not have believed it had I not seen it for myself."

"Can you try to connect with them while this is going on?" Adia asked.

Iella said nothing, just closed her eyes and reached down inside to the place where she found the Connection with Etera's fellow creatures.

She focused on the rabbit, wanting to see what it was experiencing. Was it afraid of the fox but somehow transfixed and unable to run away? Slowly, she began to join with its consciousness. She could feel the moist moss underneath its paws and the new grass tickling its belly. Its little nails pierced the moss, and its foot pads were enjoying the coolness. Her senses were augmented, and she could hear sounds she had never imagined. Some creature burrowing underground, perhaps a mole? Bird song coming from far away. The soft breeze ruffled the hair inside the rabbit's long ears. Her nose picked up not just the sweet smell of the damp moss but also the woody fragrance of the tree bark, the scent of rotting leaves, and the smell coming off the warm body of the fox.

Iella merged deeper and was overcome with an emotion she was not expecting. It was so very strong. Suddenly she was jolted out of the Connection, and her eyes flew open.

"Oh my!" she exclaimed, and Adia reached out and touched her arm.

"Are you alright? You were so still and quiet and so peaceful, and then all of a sudden, you startled awake!"

"Adia, I need a moment." Iella covered her face in her hands.

"I am sorry. It was just so— So powerful. Oh, Adia, I know why they come to An'Kru. It is the most compelling feeling I have ever experienced. They come because they love him."

"They love him?" she repeated, at a loss for other words.

"At first, I was just feeling what the rabbit was experiencing, and taking in what it was hearing, smelling, feeling. Then I moved to a deeper Connection, and I hit what I would only describe as a well. A well of deep, abiding love like nothing I could have imagined. It was so compelling, so strong that I feared I would lose myself in it.

"I know that sounds odd," Iella continued. "Why would someone resist such a feeling of love? But it was— No, there are just no words. I was not afraid of it; I wanted to join with it more than anything. Maybe it was because it was so overpowering that somehow my spirit could not adjust to it. But that is what happens. They come to him because they love him—or because he loves them. Wherever it originates, I do not know.

"I wish I could describe it to you. It feels like being one with everything as if there is no separation —that we are all connected, woven together. I only felt it for an instant, but in that instant, time had no meaning. Nothing did. It was an experience of timelessness and connection without limit. They come to me because I ask them, but they come to him because there is no other place they want to be."

"Was it like a current?" Adia asked.

"That is a great question," Iella answered. "No, it did not have a direction. It did not move; it just was."

Adia waited patiently.

"I did not leave of my own accord, Adia," she said. "The Connection was broken somehow. I realize it now because I did not want to separate from it. I wanted never to leave. Something—or *someone*—disconnected me from the experience."

An'Kru turned his head to look up at Iella.

"No, it could not be— Could it?" she said, staring at An'Kru. "It could not have been An'Kru who broke the Connection, could it?"

In disbelief, she turned to Adia, who replied, "He is still just a very young offling, but perhaps someone else did."

Neither female speculated any further, but it was a question that would haunt them both for many years.

An'Kru turned his head back to the animals sitting quietly in front of him. Then, as if on cue, the birds who had alighted in the trees took flight, and the little creatures on the ground started to wander off, one by one. Last to leave were two does and their fawns, who had assembled themselves at the back. Adia felt as if she could almost hear the communication between them and her son, though her mind rejected it as an impossibility. An'Kru was too young to be able to talk, and he was using only the most rudimentary Handspeak.

Ned was learning quickly now that he had a basic grasp of the Brothers' language. Awantia was a patient and wise teacher, and the more time they spent together, the more he found he enjoyed her company. Despite the continued angry stares from Sakinay, Ned spent his evenings at Awantia and Myrica's fire, all of them feasting on whatever he had hunted that day. He didn't have to provide for the two women; no one went without because the Brothers took care of their own in all ways. He did it to thank them and repay the village for their help.

He had become an adept hunter, so much so that he was invited out with the other village men on their hunting parties. He learned more about how to stalk and trap than he had ever learned at his parents' farm. Only occasionally would they ever come across evidence that the Sassen were still in the area, but they were. And whereas before, the thought of some undiscovered race of people living in the woods would have terrified him, now it brought him comfort and a sense of ease.

For the most part, the conversation around Myrica and Awantia's fire was light-hearted. Sometimes the parents of one or both would join them. Often, being an avid admirer of Myrica's cooking,

Kele would show up. One particular night Ned was watching how patient Awantia was with the young boy and broached a personal topic with her.

"You are so good with children. Do you not want children of your own?"

Myrica looked over at Awantia, watching her closely to see her reaction.

Awantia lowered her eyes and fidgeted, then picked at her helping while she answered. "Of course. When the time is right, it will happen."

"Both of you are grown women; should you not be bonded by now?"

Myrica shot him a look of astonishment, which Ned caught. "Forgive me. I should not ask you such personal questions. I apologize if I crossed a line."

Awantia tossed the leavings of her meal to the side and said, "Do you feel sorry for me, Ned Webb? Yes, someday I want to have children, a life-walker, a family, but all the children of the village are mine to love and care for. I am satisfied with my lot in life."

"Again, I am sorry. I am sure there are many men who would want to—"

But Awantia stood up and left.

Myrica got up, clearly annoyed, and also walked off. Ned felt terrible. They all had such a good relationship, and now he had made a big blunder.

"I'm sorry, truly. Please forgive me," Ned called after them as they retreated into the distance. Then he stood and walked off, feeling sick to his stomach.

The next day, he sought out Tiponi and told her

what he had done and asked why it had upset his friends so much.

"A man does not usually speak of such things unless he is proposing an arrangement," Tiponi explained.

"Do you mean they thought I was trying to ask one of them to bond with me?"

"Or both; yes."

Ned's face started to burn. "Both? As in both of them—with me?"

"Awantia and Myrica have been as close as sisters since childhood, and they are almost inseparable. It is not uncommon among many of our people for a man to have more than one life-walker. It is a personal choice, and no doubt they thought that was what you were proposing," Tiponi explained.

"I was not proposing that. I was just making conversation."

"You probably should not make such conversation, then. Whatever the reason is, they did not like it."

Ned didn't know what to do. He decided he would not go near the two for a while, though, each day, he left what he had hunted for them to find the next morning. He was sad and lonely and kept to himself in his shelter, leaving only to join the braves who were going out to hunt each morning. He would occasionally glance in Awantia or Myrica's direction but looked away if he thought they noticed.

After a few days, Awantia said to Myrica, "We have punished him long enough, do you not think?"

"What do you mean punished him? And by *him*, you mean the Waschini?"

"Yes. He did not realize he was being rude; he was just wondering. It is not anything everyone in the village has wondered—why you are not bonded."

"I do not know. Maybe I thought he was leading up to something. That he was hinting about him and me. And I am tired of people questioning me about it. You do not know what it is like to know people are talking about you, asking why you are not bonded yet."

Myrica's words stung. It was true; Awantia did not know what it was like because no one was surprised she had not bonded. She was not the natural beauty Myrica was. To be fair, she had never encouraged any of the men either, not even when they went to group gatherings. She kept to herself. Her mother was always chiding her about it, saying she wanted grandchildren and to stop being so fussy. That a woman needed a man at her fire, and if she waited too long, her childbearing years would end. That she would forever be alone and dependent on the village for companionship that would never be the companionship a life-walker could give. But Awantia knew that Myrica could have had any man she wanted. In addition to her looks, she was a good cook, frugal, and knew how to put to use every last bit of a kill.

"Even you, my friend," Myrica said heatedly. "You chide me constantly about this Waschini. If you think he is so wonderful, then you can have him."

Awantia waited for her friend's temper to calm down. Yes, it was a sore spot, and poor Ned had walked right into it, but Awantia felt sorry for him. She knew he was hurting and probably didn't even understand what he had done wrong. She was not totally sure herself, only that it was a sensitive topic for Myrica, to be sure. However, Awantia had her own reasons for finding his questions upsetting.

CHAPTER 10

The Lulnomia community had accepted Moart'Tor as one of their own. He was welcomed wherever he went. He remained in his neutral-territory quarters as he found it suited him, and they were starting to feel like his. He'd had to adjust to the loss of the familiar, and it surprised him how much that impacted him. Each time he walked down a tunnel or through an outside area, he assured himself it would become more and more familiar as time passed, and eventually, it would feel like home.

Moart'Tor wondered what had happened to the fire within him that had burned at the thought of taking a female. At Zuenerth, it was the biggest reward any male could receive. He was perplexed that the thought of being paired did not bring him more joy. The females he had met were pleasant, comely, sturdy, and promised many healthy offling, but one seemed much the same as another. He knew he would never return home, that his life was here. But he wondered if perhaps leaving everything he had ever known had affected him more than he realized. He was no doubt mourning the loss of his family, misguided though they were. He did often wonder about his mother and father and his siblings, and he would forever long for them to have the change of heart that would let them join him among the other Mothoc. But there was no turning back. Moart'Tor knew he would spend the rest of his life here and that the others were right; taking a mate would help him move forward into the future of his own making.

Irisa approached him one morning at first meal.

"I have good news. Females from the House of 'Yow and the House of 'Azye have both offered to pair with you. If they appeal to you, now you have only to decide which to accept."

Moart'Tor put down the root he had been chewing on and wiped his mouth with the back of his hand. "How long do I have to decide?"

"It is a big decision, and of course, you must be sure of your choice but try not to take too long; they and their families are waiting."

The enormity of it sank in. Those females had both expressed how much they wanted offling—and sooner rather than later. It would be uncomfortable to be kept waiting, and no doubt the one he did not choose would be disappointed, as would her family.

Moart'Tor was seen as a very desirable male due to his unique coloring and his relationship to the Guardian Pan.

"I will decide shortly, I promise."

He considered the two females. Both were attractive enough. Coho from the House of 'Yow was younger and therefore would have a longer fertile period, more stamina, and perhaps more centuries of good health. She seemed amiable and polite, and he did not see any of his mother's highly strung personality. Her mother, however, seemed a little overzealous about the possibility of their pairing, which made Moart'Tor wonder how much of her zeal was because of his notoriety. As for Naha from the House of 'Azye, she was closer to his age and seemed calmer. Conversation between them came easier than it did with Coho. Naha also seemed to have a more seasoned outlook on life, probably because she was older.

Moart'Tor was smart enough to know that existing family relations had an impact on a pairing, so, in the end, Naha won out. Partly because of her more mature personality, but also because Coho's mother's enthusiasm reminded him a little too much of his own mother's zeal, and he didn't want that influence in his life. She had also seemed impressed by his relationship to the Guardian Pan. He wondered if perhaps she thought it might put her in a position of influence. He loved his mother, Visha, but her head had always been turned by status, and it was not an influence he wanted for his offling. However, Naha's mother seemed quiet—reticent even—and humble, and he thought, less likely to insert herself into their pairing.

As promised, he let Irisa know as soon as he had made up his mind.

Naha's family was overjoyed at the news as it meant their daughter would likely soon have offling of her own to expand the family circle. Naha herself was also happy with the prospect of being a mother. As to be expected, Coho and her family were disappointed, and Moart'Tor felt sorry for them.

He had kept Pan informed of his progress.

"You are happy with your decision?" she asked him. "Were you carried along by the enthusiasm of the others and possibly made it too quickly?"

"Naha will make a fine mother and mate. Irisa, who knows both families very well, assured me that I had made a solid choice. In time, the companionship between us will develop."

"The more time you spend with her, the more you will discover common ground, and if this is what you want, I am pleased for you, son of my brother," Pan said.

"Just as I am that you have reunited with your beloved. You are much happier than when we first came here."

"I do my best not to allow myself to grieve the lost years and rather to stay focused on the years we have ahead together. And I am getting to know my daughter, Tala. She is a fine young female. I was puzzled that she is not very interested in being paired, but I have made peace with it."

"If only my father had not poisoned the minds of those at Zuenerth," Moart'Tor said. "There are many males and females who would no doubt be able to pair with those here, and they could be happy among this Mothoc community."

"It is my fervent hope that the Great Spirit will make a way for those at Zuenerth to awaken to the truth and turn from their intention to destroy the Akassa and the Sassen. If they had a true change of heart, they would be welcome here, as you are."

"I see no way for that to happen, Guardian," Moart'Tor said sadly.

"We will not lose hope. If there is a way, the Order of Functions will provide the path forward. The will of the Great Spirit is for unity, love, and acceptance, wherever it is possible."

After Pan left, Moart'Tor went to his quarters and lay on his sleeping mat, thinking. What would it take to open the eyes of those back at Zuenerth? Could anything? Or were they so fiercely entrenched in their distorted beliefs that nothing would reach them? But he had been as they were, and his eyes were opened. Even though he did not see a way, he would keep hoping, just as Pan was doing.

At the next full moon, Moart'Tor and Naha were joined at a simple ceremony performed by Irisa in her capacity as Overseer. Naha was from the Little Rocks community and would move into his living quarters. Perhaps after they had offling, they would move to be closer to her mother and father, but she believed it was best for their budding relationship not to be embedded at the center of the Little Rocks section. The distance would give them room to find out who they were together, without her community identity overshadowing their new relationship.

After the ceremony, Moart'Tor and Naha retired to his quarters. He was relieved to find his ardor arose when they were alone together and the prospect of mating a female had become a reality. His gaze followed her as she walked about the room, checking this and that. All the living quarters were primarily the same, so since he believed it was also her expectation that they would consummate their pairing immediately, he saw this as her way to build up to the mating act.

He patiently waited for her to finish running her hand along the various surfaces, noticing the small appointments he had added to make the place his own. A few particularly beautiful rocks he had found, an eagle's feather. She finally stopped over to the sleeping mat, and he watched her lie down and stretch out before beckoning him over.

He joined her on the mat, and she drew him down. Her lips were soft and yielding, and the warmth of her skin, the scent rising up from her, jolted to life his desire. Despite all the detailed techniques the males had talked of at the rebel camp about how to arouse and satisfy a female, he found his good intentions lost. He took her quickly and deeply. Then again. Throughout the night, he mated her repeatedly, as if the stored-up years of deprivation demanded their due. She did not complain, though mid-morning, she did ask if she might be left to sleep.

"I have been inconsiderate. I apologize."

"You do not need to. Each time we mate, it is one more chance for me to become seeded. My dream of having offling lives and dies with you, Moart'Tor. I just need a little sleep, that is all."

"May I get you something first? A drink? Some dried figs, perhaps?"

"Thank you, but I will get it myself." Naha rose and went into the personal care area, then to the food counter, where she ate a few figs and took a long drink from one of the water gourds. Then she crawled back onto the sleeping mat and closed her eyes.

Moart'Tor pulled a comforting hide up over her.

He should have been tired, but he was not. Unsure of what to do while his mate slept, he rose and left to walk the halls of his new home.

Wrollonan'Tor waited for Pan's return from discharging her duties at Lulnomia. The loneliness that had been his constant companion for thousands of years was returning. He had gotten used to Pan's presence and enjoyed her company. They had talked about anything and everything, and she had been a bright and eager student who asked insightful and probing questions to make sure she understood everything he was teaching her.

But now that Pan was reunited with Rohm'Mok, her visits to him had been brief and perfunctory. Each time, it was clear she wanted to rush back to resume the life that had been abbreviated by the call of her duty as Guardian.

Irisa still came home to her father on and off. She answered his questions but did not always volunteer any information. She knew he had the ability to view whatever he wished and that if he wanted to know what was going on, he had only to create the intention.

"Moart'Tor has taken a mate," she said. "But of course, you knew that."

"No, I did not. I have been occupied with other things."

"Would you like me to tell you about it then?"

"No, I am content with not knowing. It is not a matter of much consequence; it is enough to know that he has settled into life at Lulnomia," Wrollonan'Tor replied.

"Father—"

Wrollonan'Tor put his hand up to shush her.

"Do not worry about me, my daughter. I have lived with loneliness for thousands of years, and a few more are not going to kill me, though sometimes I think it would be a kindness if they did."

Wrollonan'Tor saw the pain pass over his daughter's face and regretted his words. "I have never been very good at hiding things from you, have I? Yes, I miss Pan's companionship, but I had to accept long ago that any joy coming into a Guardian's life, though it is a blessing beyond measure, is temporary. Ours is a life of duty and responsibility, and she deserves to enjoy whatever happiness comes her way."

"I will leave you, then," Irisa said. "Is there any message you want me to take back to Pan?"

Wrollonan'Tor thought for a moment. "Yes. The years until she goes to the High Rocks and returns with the Promised One will pass quickly. Tell her to enjoy her happiness and return here only when she is ready."

Haaka had decided. She had mulled her idea over for some time and knew this was what she wanted to do and that now was the time. She and her mate were just sitting down to the meal she had prepared when she said, "It is time, Haan."

He looked up from picking through his greens for his favorites to eat first. "For what?"

"I want to have an Akassa's offling, so Kalli will not be the only one of her kind."

She watched her mate chew very slowly before he answered. "You mentioned this before. If that is what you want, we must speak with Acaraho and Adia. As you have said, the Ancients managed it with the Brothers; surely there will be an Akassa male willing to help you."

As Haaka had mentioned it before, Adia also knew this day would come. And some time ago, she had a flash of insight about how, using the Dream World, the Ancients might have accomplished what they had. If they could find a male willing to provide his seed, it might be an indelicate conversation, but the Healers were willing to endure it for Haaka and Kalli's sake. Adia would explain the process to Haaka, and Artadel, Haan's Healer, would explain the male's part of it to the Akassa male concerned.

It was not hard to figure out the basics, only how to get the male's seed into Haaka. Adia called Nadiwani and Iella together, and after much discussion, they came up with a method. Whether it was how the Ancients had done it or not, no one would ever know. But they were fairly satisfied it would work well enough.

Acaraho spoke with his males in private and explained that Haaka had no expectation for whoever volunteered also to be part of the offspring's life. He then explained why she wanted to do this, for little Kalli's sake. Finally, he sent them off and said that if anyone would be willing, they should let him know privately.

Later Acaraho told Adia that, to his surprise, several had come forward.

"That is great news, and just as well, as she may not become seeded at first."

"That thought had occurred to me. And with several volunteers, Haaka will not know who the father truly is, then," he added.

"I do not know if that is a benefit or not. I did not think to ask Haaka, but now I feel I must. What of the offspring; will he or she want to know at some point? Will he or she not have a right to know who—?"

Adia glanced up at the rock ceiling. "Nimida. This is no different in many ways from Nimida's situation. Of course, the offspring will want to know who its father is. I must speak with Haaka, and we must rethink this. Perhaps there should be only one male involved because we must also consider the future offspring's feelings."

Haaka listened carefully and agreed with Adia. "In my desire to ensure Kalli would not be alone, I had not thought of this, so thank you; I could have made my offling's life complicated. The male does not have to be further involved, as I said, but I owe it to the soul I am trying to bring into our realm to know who seeded him or her."

That night, Adia could not sleep. She had realized before that Nimida had a right to know who her father was, but now she understood it at a far deeper level. She feared Nimida's knowing the truth would hurt her, and though Adia accepted that there would be an emotional impact to hearing the rest of the story, it soothed her to know that on some level, it would satisfy a need that everyone had, the need to know who their mother and father were. She must speak with Khon'Tor at the earliest opportunity. He had a right to know that she felt she must tell Nimida the rest of the story.

Khon'Tor was meeting with Harak'Sar and Brondin'Sar. He was explaining how Oh'Dar and his grandmother were teaching the People at the High Rocks how to read and write Whitespeak. He told them he had initially asked Oh'Dar to do this because they had learned that their history as it had been told to them was wrong, and they needed a more trustworthy way of recording events. Whitespeak was able to capture and convey precise information that could be accessed by anyone who could read it.

Harak'Sar listened carefully, and both he and his son agreed it should also be done at the Far High Hills. So Khon'Tor set out for Kthama to speak with Acaraho.

Both Adia and Acaraho were present.

"When you are ready for it to happen, Harak'Sar is willing to send someone here to the High Rocks to be taught Whitespeak, and when they are knowledgeable, they will return to the Far High Hills and begin teaching our people there."

"It was your idea, to begin with, Khon'Tor, and it was a great one," Acaraho said. "Without hesitation, I can speak for the willingness of Oh'Dar and Miss Vivian to teach one of Harak'Sar's people. Or as many as he wishes to send."

"Then, if that is acceptable, I will stay a few days to speak with Oh'Dar and his grandmother and start putting ideas together."

He turned to Adia. "I also came to ask on behalf of Urilla Wuti how Iella is doing."

"I know she is in the Healer's Quarters as I left her a few moments ago. I will be glad to take you to her," Adia offered, "and you may speak with her yourself."

Khon'Tor and Adia left the meeting room. They walked together in silence for a while, Khon'Tor following a step behind down a particularly narrow tunnel. Then Adia stopped and turned back to face him. "I am glad you are here. It is good timing, really. I need to let you know that Nimida wants to know who seeded her, and I believe she has a right to know. But I also know it may cause— Well, I do not know what it may cause, but you understand what I am trying to say," she stammered.

"Of course. Her brother knows, and it is only fair that she should, too. I have wondered if this day would come, and no matter how often I turned it over in my imagination, I never came up with an easy scenario."

Adia cast her eyes downward.

"None of this is your fault, Healer. No matter what the outcome, you must remember that. It was I who wronged you so terribly. Whatever the repercussions are, they are mine to bear." He paused. "And, unfortunately, also Tehya's, but she knows what I did, and she knew this day might come. I have hurt many people, none of whom deserved it, and for that, I will be eternally sorry."

"Nimida said she would let me know when she is ready to learn who it is," said Adia. "I have no way of knowing how soon or how far off that may be."

"Thank you for letting me know."

Nimida and Tar continued on with their day-to-day lives. Her emotions rose and fell with no particular pattern. There were days when she felt almost like her old self, then there were days when she was filled with regret over the loss of the life she could have had there at Kthama. Other days, she wished she had never found out the truth, but mostly, she was happy she had, no matter how hard moving forward had become.

"You are having a good day," Tar observed.

"Yes, today is a good day. Perhaps we should go do something fun! The first fruits of spring are bearing."

Tar rose and reached up to the peg her harvesting basket was hanging from. "It is early; we can get a start before the sun's rays heat up."

Soon, stains coated their fingertips as they picked dark blue berries. They ate as many as made it into the basket, which they chuckled about. Nimida pointed at her mate and laughed at the blue stains on his lips. They stuck their tongues out at each other and laughed even harder. When they'd had enough, they wandered down to a little eddy and washed their hands as best they could. Then they sat down on the bank, and both lay back and stared up at the beautiful blue sky, broken up only by a few puffy clouds drifting slowly by.

Nimida reached over and took Tar's hand. "Thank you for standing by me through everything. I know it has been difficult."

"It has been hard on you. I am so sorry, and I pray that in time it will become easier to bear."

"I believe it will," Nimida said. "I have decided I am ready to find out who my father was. Is."

"Whoever it is, we will go through this together. Maybe finding out will give you another piece of the puzzle. Have you decided what you will do when you find out who it is? Will you confront him?"

"Oh, I just do not know. I go back and forth. I think I want to, then other times I think I do not. Maybe who it is will make the difference." She pushed herself up to look at her mate. "I have realized that I did not stop to think it might be someone you know—or knew. It must have been someone who was here at Kthama, right?"

Tar answered, "I kept to myself for most of my life. It is possible I would not know him, whoever it was. But if I do, I will tell you."

Scooting closer Nimida snuggled up against him. He put his arm around her, and they dozed for a little while under the wide blue canopy overhead.

Nimida dreamt she was looking for someone. She was walking down first one of Kthama's tunnels, then another. She could hear someone walking ahead of her, their footfalls loud enough to follow. Somehow she knew it was a male, and she knew he was tall and powerfully built. The footsteps would start and stop, and each time she thought she was almost upon him, she rounded a corner, and no one was there. It was a dream she'd had many times since learning the truth about her past.

Nimida stirred, and Tar gently shook her awake. "You are having that dream again, yes?"

Nimida wiped her eyes and sat up a bit. "Yes, the same one; I guess it will not go away until I find out who he is. I truly do not know why I am putting it off."

Tar got up and helped her to her feet. They brushed the small grasses and leaves off themselves and headed back to the High Rocks.

When they entered Kthama, Adia, Acaraho, the High Protector, Awan, and another male Nimida recognized as Khon'Tor, the former Leader of the High Rocks, were talking just inside. Nimida glanced over at Adia as she walked. She did not want to interrupt them and certainly would not say anything to Adia in front of anyone else.

When Nimida and Tar walked by, Adia knew. Nimida was ready to find out who had seeded her.

CHAPTER 11

Riggs was more than ready to leave his sister's home. Over the past weeks, he had completed all the odd jobs he had started. Then he gathered his personal belongings together and readied his horse. Mary had baked him some goodies for the trip and washed out and dried all his clothes, while John and the boys had helped him with supplies for the trip. With his saddlebags packed, Riggs said his goodbyes and rode out, heading toward Chief Is'Taqa's village.

It might have seemed odd to anyone else that Riggs would set out to the one place he should not have gone. There was no doubt the scouts around the village would see him coming long before he arrived, and they would recognize him and most likely alert Grayson Morgan. However, Riggs counted on all of it happening just like that. Grayson Stone Morgan would come to him, and he was ready.

"A message has been brought by one of our watchers from the far end of Chief Is'Taqa's territory," High Protector Awan told Acaraho. "A Waschini rider is approaching, and they are confident it is the one they call the constable, the one who tried to abduct Snana and Noshoba. He is headed in the direction of their village."

"Oh, how I hate to tell Oh'Dar this. It seems all my son does anymore is deal with Waschini problems. Alright, I will find him. I know he will want to ride over to the village and handle it himself."

It took a while to locate him, and Acaraho had to ask several people, but he finally found Oh'Dar with his grandparents. Acise and I'Layah were there, and the five of them were visiting together. Miss Vivian was sewing something while Acise and I'Layah were sitting playing on the floor. Ben was in his usual place with his leg propped up, and Oh'Dar was sitting on a chair next to his grandmother.

Acaraho hated to break up the conversation, but Oh'Dar would want to know. He told them about the visitor.

Acise reached up and grabbed Oh'Dar's hand. He leaned over, raised her hand to his lips, and kissed it. "I will leave right away. I will not let him harm your family or anyone else. Please do not worry."

Before he left, Oh'Dar stopped by his quarters to retrieve Ben's pistol. As much as he hated to, he had tucked the pistol into the waist of his leggings where it was covered by his tunic.

He didn't know how much time he had to get there, but he wanted to be at the village before Riggs arrived. He knew the watcher would also have alerted Chief Is'Taqa's scouts that the man was coming.

When he arrived, the village was empty of women and children, even though it was in the middle of the day. Honovi, Snana, and Noshoba had been cloistered in one of the shelters furthest away, presumably where they were less likely to be seen.

"I am sorry that I am causing more trouble for you," Oh'Dar said to the Chief.

"It is not you who is causing the trouble; the Waschini constable is causing the trouble. We will see what he wants this time."

"I am surprised he keeps at it. A wise man would have dropped whatever this vendetta is against me and moved on. But whatever it is, it must be something serious for him to risk coming here again."

With as many precautions in place as possible, including getting the women and children safely out of sight, the men waited until, finally, Riggs' horse came into view.

None of the men moved, so Riggs rode up to them, pulled his horse around, and dismounted.

"You knew I was coming," he said to Oh'Dar.

"Why are you here? I would have thought the Governor made it clear you were to stay away?"

"I don't work for the Governor any longer, and this is between you and me and no one else." Riggs shot a glare at the Chief, Pajackok, and the other braves standing nearby.

"Say what you have come here to say," Oh'Dar said.

"Alone," Riggs shot back brusquely.

They stepped away and Riggs looked back before speaking. "You ruined my life. You cost me my career. I could have been Governor one day, but now that is an impossibility. I have no way to make a living, so since it's your fault I'm in this position, you are going to pay."

"Why would I do that? Your predicament is your own doing. Ever since the trial ended, you have followed my family and me, trying to make trouble. And as for your position with the Governor, you knew Chief Kotori's village was on my property."

"I knew you would not take responsibility, Morgan, so I will make it clear for you. Either you provide me with a nice annuity like the one I hear you set up for the Webb children, or I will reveal what is really going on up here."

Oh'Dar chuckled involuntarily. "And what is that exactly?"

"Your grandmother is—or was—very wealthy. No one walks away from that lifestyle without a serious reason, so don't tell me that she and her new husband just wanted to change their lives. Rubbish. Something is going on up here, something you don't want anyone to know about. I know what I heard and what Tucker and his men heard, and it wasn't natural. No creature on earth makes that sound. Everyone knows Ben Jenkins is a breeding expert, and you don't seem to care about genetic purity. You are, for whatever reason, breeding monsters up here."

"That is preposterous," Oh'Dar replied.

"Is it? Maybe it is, maybe it isn't. But I know the last thing you want is a whole lot of people up here snooping around. Everyone loves a good mystery. If you want me to keep my mouth shut, you had better get with your lawyer and set me up. Otherwise, I will make sure the Monsters of the Morgan Trust becomes the biggest witch hunt of the century."

Oh'Dar thoughtfully rubbed his chin. "So you are blackmailing me with some ridiculous story about monsters. You will be the laughingstock of the century; that is all that will come out of it."

"Are you willing to take that chance? If you do as I say, it won't cost the Morgan Trust but a pittance of the Morgan wealth. If you don't, your gamble could cost you everything."

"You really believe Ben Jenkins and I are

breeding—what did you say—*monsters*? For what purpose?"

"It doesn't matter whether I believe it; it only matters whether others do. And why? I don't know. You seem to favor the locals over your own race. Maybe you plan on eliminating all of us, so your beloved friends can have it all."

"I need some time; I will have to go to Wilde Edge to have my lawyer make arrangements."

"I'll give you two weeks. I expect to hear from you by that time, or I'll start my campaign to fill these woods with all types of glory-hunting fanatics. A big reward motivates people, you know."

"You just said you have no money. What big reward are you offering?" Oh'Dar asked.

"Doesn't matter if I have the money or not; they'll come believing I do. And, besides, it's my problem. Yours will be keeping your secrets just that. I will see you in two weeks; that should give you enough time to make your arrangements, and I'll be waiting for you in Wilde Edge."

Riggs put out his hand.

Oh'Dar didn't return the gesture. "I don't shake hands with blackmailers."

Riggs smirked and shrugged. Then he mounted his horse and rode off.

Oh'Dar watched him ride away, his mind running at full speed. Riggs could cause a lot of trouble, and though he was wrong about his and Ben's activities, the rest of the world would consider both the Akassa and the Sassen to be monsters. Was it a bluff he was willing to take? He had to talk to Storis.

So, once again, Oh'Dar made the ride to Wilde Edge.

The Webbs were glad to see him, though he could see the disappointment on their faces that Ned had not also come. He met with Storis, and they started planning how to take care of Riggs.

Khon'Tor was still at the High Rocks, but with Oh'Dar called away, he had decided to head back to the Far High Hills.

As was usually the case when he visited Kthama, many people wanted to speak with him. Some wanted to reminisce, while others had a genuine interest in hearing about his life with Tehya and their offspring at the Far High Hills. Some just wanted to be able to say they knew him, as he was still a legend among the People.

He disciplined himself not to look for Nimida in the comings and goings of people throughout the cave system. He had not spoken with Adia since the first day he arrived, and he had no idea if Nimida knew the truth yet or not. So, it caught him off guard when she and Tar approached him.

"Adik'Tar, my mate has something to give you." He turned to Nimida.

She held out a blade. "I have found a way to

bind the handles more securely to the blades, along with some other subtle changes. I wanted you to have one in case you would like me to teach this new technique to your toolmakers at the Far High Hills."

Khon'Tor took the blade. "This is excellent handiwork. Thank you, I am sure they will be interested. I will make sure they come to the next High Council meeting and make time to meet with you."

"I am glad to be of service," she said as he handed the blade back to her.

When Nimida and Tar left, Khon'Tor realized his heart was pounding. He had thought he was ready to face things with her, but apparently not. He expected her to be angry when the time came, and he had thought he was prepared to take the brunt of her wrath, but she seemed so vulnerable just now. He wondered if he was prepared to accept how much he had impacted her life. Anger he could deal with. Hurt he was not so sure of.

As fate would have it, Nimida had decided to go that day to Adia to learn who had fathered her. She knew Adia worked every day with Iella in the Healer's Quarters, but around midday, took care of her offspring in the Leader's Quarters, so she timed her visit for when Adia would be there.

Adia was surprised when her daughter showed

up. She had just put An'Kru and the twins down for a nap and invited Nimida in to sit.

"I am ready to know who my father was. Is."

"You have a right to know. After I tell you, will you please let me explain further the circumstances surrounding what happened?"

Just then, Acaraho walked in, and Adia saw the surprised look that crossed his face.

"May Acaraho stay?" she asked. "It involves him too."

Nimida said, "I suppose so. He obviously already knows."

Acaraho chose his seat so the three would be equidistant from each other.

"It was a tumultuous time when this took place," Adia started. "The community was just learning about the Waschini threat, which the High Council had tied to ushering in the advent of the Age of Shadows, and I had only recently rescued Oh'Dar. I had broken sacred law, and Khon'Tor was taxed in trying to punish me for my disobedience without destroying the community as I had great favor with the People. In addition, his mate was harboring jealousy and resentment toward me for reasons I did not understand at the time but later discovered."

A look of confusion crossed Nimida's face.

"There is too much to try to explain," Adia sighed. "And the more I try to, the more it probably sounds as if, for some reason, I am just making excuses for what happened."

"I am confused. So far, you have only talked about the Adik'Tar and—" Nimida's jaw dropped. "Oh, no. Oh, no."

"Yes," Adia said. "Your father is Khon'Tor, former Leader of the High Rocks."

"He did that? He took you Without Consent?" Nimida leaped up from her seat and paced around. "The Leader of the High Rocks? How is that possible? Of anyone, how could he do that?"

"As I said, there is too much to try to explain. He did it in a fit of rage. He was out of his mind at the time, I truly believe, driven there by many factors."

"Are you defending him? He is a rapist, and you are making excuses for what he did?"

"No, I am not. That is what I was afraid you would think. I suppose, in some strange way, because he is your father, I don't want you to think badly of him."

Nimida wiped her hand across her face. "Why was he not punished? Or is that why he left the High Rocks? No, that cannot be right; there was too much time in between—unless no one knew?"

"For a long time, no one knew. Everyone thought Acaraho was the father and that we had broken my Healer's vow of chastity. It was not until Nootau was old enough to be paired that the truth came out."

Nimida's face paled. "Nootau and I talked about this, how the High Council selected us for each other, and we were nearly paired. So *you* stopped it."

"Yes. There is more behind it, but, yes, ultimately,

I had to tell the High Council that Khon'Tor was your father and not Acaraho as everyone believed."

"He denied it?"

"No. He did not deny it; he confessed to it. Something changed in him. Shifted. He had true remorse. He is not the same person who committed that grievous crime against me. And as for punishment, the High Council wanted to banish him."

"I have never heard he was banished. How did he return to the High Rocks?" Nimida turned her gaze to Acaraho. "I only know that he left after he stepped down and you took over."

"Your mother stopped the High Council from banishing him for the same reason she hid the truth all those years. To save the community, she bore the pain and shame of what he did to her. If the People had been told, there could have been civil war, and not just at the High Rocks. Not everyone would have believed Adia, and lines would have been drawn. It was a fragile time for all the People, and many would have lost faith in him as a Leader at a time when they needed him most. Your mother sacrificed her right to justice for the sake of everyone else."

"I need to think about this. I— I understand something of what you are saying, Acaraho."

She turned to Adia, "I just need time. Does— Does Khon'Tor know you were going to tell me?"

"Yes. Only not when that would be."

"Tar and I spoke with him earlier this morning," Nimida reflected. "I think I now understand why you kept it a secret, and if you believed it was important enough to do so, I will not undo whatever good you thought it would do to let him get away with what he did. But," she added. "I cannot promise I will not confront him about it."

Adia rose and walked over to her daughter. "No one could ask you to do that, Nimida."

They looked at each other a moment, and then, silently, Nimida left.

Acaraho said to his mate, "I do not pretend to know how hard that was. You are the strongest soul I have ever known."

"I did what I thought was in line with our first law, that the needs of the community come before the needs of the one. I have no way of knowing how it would have turned out if I had acted differently," Adia said. "Either way, people would have been hurt."

"Saraste', I know something of what you went through. You did what you thought best for everyone involved, and you know that better than anyone—or at least you should."

Adia shook her head. "In all of this, there is only one person whose every action should be applauded, and that is you. You willingly shared the brunt of the blame, you raised both Nootau and Oh'Dar as your own, and you never defended yourself against the judgmental talk and scathing glances. You did not have to do any of that. It was your standing with me that led people to believe you were the father, and that is a debt I can never repay."

Nimida had every intention of going for a long walk outside Kthama to clear her mind, but as she was partway down the main path, she ran into Khon'Tor, who was coming up.

"Oh. It's you," she said.

Khon'Tor stopped. "Were you looking for me?"

"No. Not this minute, although one day I would have been. But yes. Yes, in some way, I guess I was."

She waited for him to say something, but he didn't. Then she wanted to run but knew she would feel terrible later if she did.

Finally, he spoke. "Nimida, have you spoken to Adia lately?"

She felt a flash of gratitude that he seemed to be opening a way for her to say what she needed to. "Yes. I just came from talking to her and Acaraho."

"I understand you have been talking to her about your past."

"I know—" Nimida looked around to be sure no one was approaching. "I know— Who you are," she stammered.

"For what it is worth, I am sorry—not for being your father, but for how it came about. There is nothing I can do to make up for what I did; I know that, and you have every right to be angry with me, with the entire situation."

He was being so kind, and it should have been a relief, but it was making things harder. Then she realized she wanted to yell at him, tell him what a terrible person he was and how he had ruined her life, but he wasn't giving her a reason to.

"She tried to explain what other things were going on at that time," Nimida said.

"Well, there were a lot. It was a complicated time, and several factors worked together to bring about what I did. But it was utterly reprehensible, and ultimately, the responsibility is mine. Did Adia tell you about the High Council?"

"Yes. And that you did not know about me until Nootau asked to be paired." She looked at him fleetingly but had to look away. She felt exposed, vulnerable, and fragile.

"She kept you a secret, and for good reason. Perhaps, in time, it will all make more sense. Not for my sake, but for your own and your brother's," Khon'Tor said.

"I want to hate you," she blurted out. "I was prepared to hate you."

"You have every right to. No one, including me, would blame you."

He leaned over to make eye contact with her. "I am not the one to counsel you because anything I say will sound self-serving—as if I am trying to excuse what I did. But I hope you will reach out to those who love you to help you through. Adia loves you, Nimida. And I know without a doubt that every decision she made was what she thought was the best for everyone involved."

"She suffered for what you did."

"She, and Acaraho. He stood by her the entire time. He took the blame for what I did."

"He knew all along?"

"From very early on, yes."

"I am surprised he did not want to kill you."

"He did. Adia forbade it, but for his sake, not mine," Khon'Tor explained.

"I have so many questions. What about your mate? Does she—?"

"She knows. She is another exceptional female. Despite my many and serious failings, I have been blessed to be surrounded by wise and forgiving souls."

Nimida was becoming so confused. "You seem so nice. So kind. How could you have done what you did?" Standing before her was not the monster she envisioned.

"I was a different person then. The person who committed that crime, and others, no longer exists."

Nimida looked around her. "I am going to go now."

"Of course; I am sure it is overwhelming."

She started to thank him for his time, but it felt so awkward that she just pushed past and went on her way down the path that led away from Kthama.

She walked and walked, not taking care where she was going. Finally, when she felt she couldn't take another step, she found a quiet and secluded place to rest for a while before turning back.

Khon'Tor made his farewells, and with Oh'Dar not being back from Wilde Edge, returned to the Far High Hills. After conferring with Harak'Sar and Brondin'Sar, he sought out his mate, who was in her workshop.

"Oh, you are home!" Tehya set aside the pattern she was working on and rushed into his arms. "Your son and daughter are with my parents. How did your visit go?"

Kweeuu the wolf, never far from her side if he could help it, raised his head and thumped his tail against the rock floor. He was older now, coming into the last years of his lifespan.

"Oh'Dar was called away, so I was not able to speak with him," Khon'Tor explained. "But as we expected, Acaraho is more than willing for anyone of Harak'Sar's choice to be trained in Whitespeak. I expect no other reaction from Oh'Dar."

He brushed stray hair from her face. "I am so glad to be home."

"I am also so glad, Adoeete," she whispered and kissed him sweetly. "I am sure my parents would be glad to keep Arismae and Bracht'Tor overnight, so we can enjoy the evening together alone." She smiled demurely.

Then her eyes searched his face. "Something is troubling you. Please tell me what it is."

"I am sorry, I did not want our reunion to be clouded by anything, but as usual, you read me too well. Something from the past has surfaced."

Tehya led him to the seating area. "Sit with me."

"You know my sins and have forgiven me for each one, Saraste', but you do not know all the repercussions. You were at the hearing when Kurak'Kahn tried me for the crimes I committed. The females I took Without Their Consent."

"Yes, I know all of this; now tell me what is troubling you," she encouraged him.

"Please believe me when I tell you I only found out much later that Adia had given birth to twins. Not just Nootau but also a daughter. For her safety, the daughter was removed from the High Rocks before anyone knew of her but the handful of people involved. She was raised elsewhere, never knowing I had seeded her or the circumstances of her birth, but some years ago, she came to the High Rocks."

"Nimida," Tehya said.

Khon'Tor was mystified. "What? How do you know? I never told you about her."

Tehya released a long breath. "Adoeete, after the trial, when Kurak'Kahn nearly killed you with the jhorallax, you were dying, and I did not want to live without you. We were both fading away until Adia rescued us. Do you remember the dream we both had? It was somehow real. Adia joined our consciousness and gave us both back the will to live. But in doing that, in some way, her memories were shared with me. I have known about Nimida for a long time."

Khon'Tor shook his head. "I do not know what to say. Why have you not spoken of this before?"

"I told you a long time ago, the person who committed these crimes no longer exists; there is none of him living in you any longer. I did not know if your daughter's existence would ever come up. If not, I had no problem with it, and if it did, I would deal with it as we always have—together."

"So you never told Adia?"

"About the transfer of her memories to me? I did not know what to say about it, so I said nothing. In the face of what we had just been through, it seemed inconsequential."

"Just when I think I know you and the depth of your compassion and understanding, you prove me wrong," he lowered his voice to almost a whisper, "and amaze me further."

"So, Nimida, does she know you are her father?"

"Yes, we spoke. She is hurting, struggling, and it is my fault," Khon'Tor said.

"Yet without what you did, she would not be alive. It has an element of tragic irony, does it not?

"After the trial at the Far High Hills, after I had confessed my crimes and after Acaraho delivered the lashes with the jhorallax, even as I thought I was dying, I felt peace. Well, at least a semblance of peace, that restitution had been made. But that was before I descended into the horror of separation and isolation from which Adia saved me. Saved us."

"I regained peace after Pan appeared, and once again, whatever Adia did for me at Kthama truly healed my inner wounds. After that, my strength and confidence returned, and I felt more my new self than I ever had before. But now that is waning, as the weight of what I did to Adia and the others becomes more and more evident to me. And Acaraho. He and Adia paid the price, and Acaraho took the blame and the shame that should have been mine. All those years and she never revealed my sin. Oh, I understand why. Her reasons were always to protect or take care of someone else, never herself."

"You do not have to keep paying for your crimes," Tehya declared.

Khon'Tor walked over to gaze down at their offspring's empty nesting areas. "We males are physically so much stronger, and we are looked up to, even sometimes revered. And yet the more I learn, the more I realize it is the females who are stronger, not us. We may have physical strength, endurance, the advantage of size, but your souls, the essence of all females, is the true strength of our realm."

"There is nothing I can say to prevent whatever you are thinking of doing, is there?"

He returned and gently took her face in his

hands. "Shame is not a punishment, Saraste'. This shame I bear shows me the way to further redemption, and I would like to set the record straight. It is not right that Adia and Acaraho live under the shadow of my crime, but I am not ignoring you. Before I take any action, I will discuss what I am thinking of with the Overseer, I promise."

Urilla Wuti listened carefully. She had been involved in nearly all of it, starting before the birth of Nootau and Nimida. She had watched Adia struggle with the High Council's decisions, first forcing her to give up either Oh'Dar or the offspring she was carrying and then intending to banish Khon'Tor. It was she who had secreted Nimida away and had her taken to the Great Pines. Through the years, Urilla Wuti had stood by Adia as she did her best to protect those she loved while bearing up under the common belief that she had failed to keep her Healer's vow of chastity.

The Overseer had also been at the trial when Kurak'Kahn tried to murder Khon'Tor to avenge the death of his niece, but though she had seen Khon'Tor change to become the male he was now, she had not witnessed first-hand the turmoil he had endured.

When he finished talking, she said, "You seek to

make right the wrongs of the past, yet you know that is impossible."

"I know I cannot undo what I did, but I also cannot continue to let the characters and honor of Adia and Acaraho be besmirched, even after all these years. And there are Nimida and Nootau to think of."

"If you decide to do this, know that it will affect Adia, Nimida, and Nootau, as well as all three mates. Be sure your motives are to help them and not to alleviate your guilt, and then, before you take any action, ask their permission."

Khon'Tor knew Urilla Wuti held no malice toward him and wanted to help. She was right; he had to make sure his intentions were pure and not self-centered and that any action would help more than it would harm. So, he decided to pray about his intentions before making a move in any direction. That, and then he would speak with Adia, Nimida, and Nootau to learn how they felt about a public confession.

CHAPTER 12

Newell had prepared everything he and Oh'Dar had discussed, and they were waiting in Newell's office for Riggs to arrive.

Though Storis had left word at the place Riggs was staying, he kept them waiting for a while. When he finally showed up, Oh'Dar indicated an empty chair and told him to sit down.

"I am glad you have come to your senses so we can all be done with each other. After this, I will go my way and not bother you again," Riggs said.

"I am sure you will," Newell replied. "Now, where do I start?" He shoved some paperwork across his desk.

Riggs picked up the top sheet, "What is this?"

"The first is a sworn statement by Sheriff Moore that you were well aware the property the locals were living on was privately owned by the Morgan Trust."

With a deep frown on his face, Riggs looked up, set it aside, and picked up the next.

"Posters the local Sheriff saved, with which you tried to track down information about any 'hairy wild men'."

Riggs took the third paper and examined it.

"Sworn statements of people you enlisted using your position as constable to illegally trespass on the Morgan Trust property in search of what you called a 'big bear', all stating that you told them you had the authority of the Governor to enlist their cooperation," Newell explained before continuing.

"The next is the sworn statement of one of the men you hired to go to the local village to abduct the wife of the Chief and any others of mixed blood while again proclaiming that you were acting under the authority of the Governor.

"There is also a statement from Commander Riley of the 14th Regiment. He confirms that you delivered orders for him to abduct any local villagers in the area when you knew full well that the area was owned by the Morgan Trust and that those people were living on privately owned property. Shall I continue?"

Riggs scowled. "So you are trying to blackmail me back?"

"This isn't blackmail. These are just the facts depicting your illegal behavior, and with which we are prepared to move forward."

"Unless I drop my request," Riggs said.

Oh'Dar spoke up. "That isn't on the table. These are crimes you committed for which you need to be held accountable, and seeing that Judge Walker will probably hear your case, your concern over your future is most likely taken care of. You will be provided for, only not in the manner you intended," he said.

"And your quest and obsession with finding the so-called tall hairy man will take care of any credibility you had left," Newell added.

"We are done here, and in case you thought of running—" Oh'Dar walked to the door and opened it.

Outside was Sheriff Moore.

Knowing it would be some time before Riggs was brought to trial, Oh'Dar returned to Kthama.

The case was indeed to be presided over by Judge Walker, and Riggs was certain of the outcome. He knew he was going to prison with or without a trial, and as much as possible, he wanted to contain the damage to himself.

Riggs' lawyer knew that the witnesses were ready to testify, including the Governor. Riggs was confident the Governor would also be only too happy to testify against him to distance himself publicly from the man he had personally selected to serve as constable.

After considering all possible outcomes and based on his lawyer's advice, Riggs pleaded no contest to the charges. These were charges of trespassing, misrepresentation, intent to commit false arrest against people, including a minor, and a slew of other charges related to his part in Commander Riley's removal of Chief Kotori's people from private land without the landowner's knowledge or consent. Judge Matthews sentenced Riggs to fifteen years in prison, the stiffest collective penalty allowed for Riggs' crimes and misdemeanors but reduced the time to ten years in exchange for the plea of no contest.

Because the case did not go to trial, there was no need for Oh'Dar to travel back to Wilde Edge. Storis instead rode to Chief Is'Taqa's village to deliver the outcome.

"Do you think we have seen the last of him?" Oh'Dar asked.

"I don't know. I suspect the Governor exerted some influence there, again not wanting the publicity. But the truth is, he might have been better off being hanged. Prisons are terrible places, and he is likely to die there. But if he does survive, the question will be, how deep is his hatred for you? Would he once more risk prison—or worse—by trying to cause you more trouble? Only time will tell."

Oh'Dar thought of his uncle Louis, who had escaped hanging, no doubt due to Miss Vivian's influence. "A waste of a life, to be sure."

The next morning, just as Newell was getting ready to head back, he said, "We haven't talked about the obvious, Grayson. That, without knowing, Riggs was right about part of it. If they had seen what Ned and I have, most people would say that there are indeed monsters living on the Morgan property."

"The Akassa and the Sassen have lived here for thousands and thousands of years, known only to the Brothers. It is only under the direst of circumstances that they risk their existence being discovered. Riggs' claims have no doubt been filed in people's minds as a man's imagination running wild. When you talked to the men he hired to look for the strange bear, as he called it, did any of them speak of any strange encounters here?"

"No, not one of them, though I got the impression one farmer and his sons were hiding something. But whatever it was, it was obvious they had no intention of telling anyone, ever."

"Then I suspect the Sassen and the Akassa will continue living in peace for thousands of years to come. At least, I hope so, for the sake of every other living creature."

"Some day, perhaps you can tell me more about them and the relationship with our planet that you alluded to. But now I need to get back home. Have you heard anything from Ned, any news I can take back?"

"No," Oh'Dar said, "but that most likely means everything is going well."

CHAPTER 13

The day was nearly over. Ned had accompanied Awantia into the forest to help her gather the tender new shoots she needed for her work. Her basket was full, and even though it was not very far to the village, they had stopped for a while before going back.

They sat on the bank of a little stream, not far from where Pakwa fished. Ned put his feet into the water and sighed at how cool it was. "It feels good after all that walking," he said. "What are the uses of everything we gathered today?"

"Most are dyes, but some are for Tiponi for healing. Others are for cooking."

"You are so wise and strong. You are skilled in many things, and your sense of humor lights even the darkest mood. Any man would be fortunate to be with you," Ned said in a moment of seriousness.

This time Awantia did not assume that he was criticizing her for not being bonded, but before continuing such a personal conversation, she looked around briefly to make sure they were alone.

"I know you do not mean to be improper by your questions, Ned Webb, so I will answer them. My mother blames my friendship with Myrica. We are always together, and all the men see is her beauty."

"It is true; she is exceptionally lovely, but that is not all that matters to all men." Seeing the look on Awantia's face, he tried again. "I did not mean you were not also beautiful."

She looked away. "I know I am not. It is not a truth I hide from myself."

"But it is not true. You do not see yourself as others see you. You *are* attractive, and even beyond that, the pureness of your spirit shines through in everything you do. You must never think for a moment that you are second to Myrica."

"I appreciate your kind words, but it does not matter to me; the village is my family, and I will be taken care of in my final years. I would rather be alone than choose someone for convenience. I made peace with that a long time ago."

"I understand, though I do not agree that you will have to be alone unless that is your choice. As for me, I doubt I will bond. Oh'Dar was a special case, but none of the Brothers would have me. It has been made clear that I am welcomed as a teacher and hunter, but I will never be one of your people."

"You speak of Sakinay's attitude toward you. That is his opinion, but he does not speak for everyone. You are a good man. Any woman would be lucky to have you at her fire."

"Again, you are being kind. But there is only one woman's fire I wish to sit at, and she shows no interest in me," he said quietly.

"I am sorry," Awantia tried to console Ned. "Myrica is my friend, and I will not speak ill of her, but I sometimes wonder why she believes as she does.

"It's not—"

"Enough of this conversation. And do be careful that no one hears us speak of these things, please?" She started to rise, "We should be getting back."

Ned stood up and leaned down to pick up Awantia's basket. As he did so, an arrow whizzed by, just missing him. It would have found its mark had he still been upright.

He quickly jerked Awantia behind him to shield her. "Who is there? Who would murder a man who has not raised a hand against him?"

Sakinay stepped out of the trees, an arrow notched in his bow. His eyes were fierce, his jaw clenched. "You came to us asking for help, and we helped you. Then you came back offering help, and we accepted you again. But, now, you betray our trust! You go too far! You have no right to this woman, Waschini!"

Sakinay raised his bow and aimed the arrow

directly at Ned's chest. At almost any distance, the brave was not likely to miss, but at this range, there was no question.

"Stop it!" Awantia leaped out from behind Ned and stormed toward Sakinay. "Stop this at once! No one has a right to me. I am my own. It is *you* who go too far, presuming to speak for me!"

"You would choose a Waschini over one of your own kind!" Sakinay shouted, not taking his eyes off Ned or lowering his aim.

"No one has chosen anyone; your anger has blinded you. And besides, what sets him apart from us except the color of his skin? Does he not hunt with our men? Does he not provide for our village, for Myrica and me? Does he not watch over the children as any of us does? He worships the same Great Spirit, and you see only the color of his skin; you are not looking at his soul."

Sakinay's arrow was still aimed directly at Ned's heart. Time seemed to stop, but keeping his eyes locked on the brave, Ned refused to look away.

Moments passed. Then slowly, Sakinay lowered his bow. Only then did Ned realize he had been holding his breath.

"Leave us," Awantia said.

Sakinay's glance moved to her, then back to Ned. He looked Ned up and down before turning and leaving.

Ned stepped forward and grasped Awantia's shoulders, "Are you alright?"

"Yes, I am."

"What do we do now?" he asked. Ned did not want to go to the Chief and complain about Sakinay, but he also didn't think it could be left unaddressed.

"Sakinay will go to Chief Kotori and admit to what he has done. He must; it is the only way to reclaim his honor."

Shaken up, they stayed a while longer until twilight had fallen.

"We should get back," Awantia said. "Myrica will wonder where we are.

They walked through the lush spring growth, and the scent of the damp soil filled their nostrils. In the distance, the peeper frogs were just starting their song. A few stars peeked out high in the sky.

Ned walked ahead but made sure Awantia was not far behind. Suddenly, a tall shape bolted out of the shadows and knocked him to the ground. Fighting to gain control, Ned frantically rolled around with the figure. It was Sakinay. He had not gone back as he should have; his anger had not faded, and he had waited there in ambush.

The two men thrashed about on the ground, knees, feet, and arms everywhere. First one had the advantage, then the other. Then Sakinay was on top with Ned pinned underneath him, an arm against Ned's throat. Ned coughed and saw Sakinay reach back to unsheathe his knife.

"No!" Awantia shouted as he wrapped his fingers around the blade's handle. As Sakinay was bringing the knife up to plunge it into Ned, She grabbed a thick fallen branch and swung it, hitting Sakinay on his arm with a resounding crack. The brave dropped the knife, but not before some damage was done. As Sakinay panted on the ground, Ned watched Awantia kick him squarely in the groin.

Having heard the commotion, Pakwa and Myrica were already on their way and came crashing through the brush, Kele behind them. Seeing Ned on the ground and Sakinay's bloody knife off to the side, they quickly surmised what had happened.

"Hurry, please; Sakinay stabbed him," Awantia cried out.

Both women dropped to their knees to see how bad the wound was.

Awantia turned to Kele. "Run and get Tiponi please!"

He took off as fast as he could while Pakwa stood over Sakinay, making sure he did not rise to attack Ned again. It was unlikely, though, as the brave was still moaning and rolling about.

It seemed only moments until others arrived.

"Oh no!" Tiponi said, and Myrica and Awantia scooted back to give her room.

Awantia's heart was pounding; she could hardly breathe. From Ned's wound, a red stream was seeping through the blades of grass into the rich soil below. Only moans and groans from him and Sakinay broke the silence as everyone waited quietly for Tiponi to speak again.

"It is not too bad," she said. "Not as bad as I feared; it is more of a shallow slash than a deep puncture, but it is bad enough. Someone run back and fetch my healing satchel and some water. Quickly!"

Tiponi then moved over to examine Sakinay. He was conscious, though still moaning. Awantia explained how she had hit him with the tree branch.

Tiponi quickly looked around. "That one?" she asked, pointing to a broken branch.

"Yes," Awantia explained, "it was the first one I could reach."

"Luckily for Sakinay, you picked a rotted one. It split in two when you hit him with it. The blow was enough to stop him but not enough to badly hurt him. No doubt his arm will ache and be badly bruised, but no permanent damage has been done," the Healer explained.

Someone returned with Tiponi's medicine satchel, and after cleaning Ned's wound, the Medicine Woman told him she had to stitch it closed. While she did so, Awantia knelt down next to Ned.

Several of the braves helped Ned and Sakinay back to the village.

Chief Kotori watched as they brought in the two

wounded men. Sakinay's father stood next to him. As the group walked by, the Chief called Awantia over. He asked her what happened, and she explained as they carefully listened.

Sakinay's father said to Awantia, "We have all seen how, in gratitude for your help, Ned Webb has taken over providing for you since he joined us. My family and I will provide for you until he is fully recovered."

Myrica had been patiently waiting while Awantia talked to Sakinay's father and the Chief. When the two friends finally had a moment together, she asked, "What prompted this?"

Awantia explained that Sakinay had taken exception to her spending so much time with Ned Webb. He had misunderstood the situation and apparently thought the Waschini was asking to be her life-walker.

"I did not know Sakinay cared for you," Myrica said. "This is a serious offense and will not be overlooked."

"I have never felt that he particularly cared for me, though he will speak on his own behalf when he is able to."

It would fall to Sakinay to provide restitution for what he had done. If he was not able to, his family would offer recompense.

Ned's wound did not become infected, but it was very sore, and because of where it was, slow to close up. Tiponi had advised him to help complete the healing by doing nothing strenuous, and it would be some time before he could do any of his usual work.

She watched carefully for any signs of fever or infection and kept him pain-free as much as possible. Kele, clearly upset, sat cross-legged outside the Medicine Woman's shelter every moment he was able, rocking and moaning to himself in grief and worry over his friend. His parents had to drag him away to care for him and get him to eat. Seeing how inconsolable he was, they were worried as much for their son's welfare as for Ned's.

Sakinay was sore from the blow Awantia had delivered. He would not speak to anyone, and they didn't know if it was out of shame for what he had done or if he was still seething with resentment toward the Waschini.

Unable to do very much, Ned had a lot of time to reflect on what had happened. He understood from overhearing others' conversations that Sakinay's attack on him was a grievous act and would not quickly be forgotten. After explaining what he wanted to say, he asked Tiponi if she would intercede on his behalf with Chief Kotori so that when the time came for Sakinay to meet with the Elders, Ned might also be allowed to speak.

In time, Sakinay did ask to see Chief Kotori and

the Elders to make a formal apology for his actions and officially declare his intended acts of restitution. Everyone expected it and was just waiting for Sakinay to come forward. Chief Kotori gathered Tiponi and the tribal Elders, and they met with the brave and his father.

"I behaved improperly," he said. "I attacked Ned Webb because I believed he and Awantia were speaking of becoming life-walkers. I have shamed myself."

The Chief and the Elders waited for him to continue. It was not their way to decide punishment or retribution; that had to come from the offender or his family.

"My father and brothers have been providing for Awantia and Myrica in the Waschini's place. I am able to take over now until the Waschini is fully healed."

Because Ned had been granted his request to speak at this council, Tiponi stepped outside and brought him into the shelter.

He looked around, seeing Sakinay and his father standing stoically next to each other. Chief Kotori nodded, indicating to Ned that he might now say what he wanted to say.

"I have come to ask forgiveness for my actions. I did not know it was not proper for me to spend so much time alone with a woman or to have such a personal conversation. It is my ignorance of your ways that led me to do so, not any intention to dishonor either Awantia of Myrica. As for Sakinay, I request tolerance for his behavior toward me. I know his skills. He could have killed me, but he waited for me to bend over before firing his arrow. It was meant only to be a warning; I am confident of this."

Unspoken was any explanation of why Sakinay then jumped Ned and tried to stab him.

When Sakinay did not speak up to defend himself, Chief Kotori turned to look at everyone else in the room and declared, "Ned Webb has proven himself in service. The hand of the Great Spirit has led him here, and he will be welcomed as one of us." Then he turned his gaze to meet Sakinay's and said, "Our words of brotherhood must be more than empty promises. If they are not, then we are no better than those who came to take us from our homes."

It was the closest thing to an admonishment that they had ever heard from the Chief. The Elders nodded in agreement. There was nothing more said, and Sakinay and his father left the meeting with not a word between them.

Tiponi motioned for Ned to follow her out, and they walked back to his shelter.

"The Chief has declared that you are one of us now," she said. "You will not be mistreated or attacked again."

"What will happen to Sakinay?" Ned asked.

"He will continue to fulfill his obligation to take over the service you were rendering to Awantia and Myrica, providing food for their fire and helping them with their work when they need it. He will not be punished; that is not our way, but he will not bother you again, I am certain."

"I have not dared talk to Awantia since this happened."

"She is worried about you, and she accepts some of the blame for what happened. You told the Chief you did not know better, which is true, but she felt she should have."

Awantia did, in part, feel responsible for Sakinay's attack. Ned hadn't known better, but she should have thought about how much time they had been spending alone together. It had also never occurred to her that one of the men in their village might become jealous as she had thought her plainness would prevent such ideas. She was sad, knowing that she had put Ned in danger.

"Perhaps it is best if Ned and I stay close to the village and do not go off together for a while. I can do my gathering alone, as I have done most of my life."

"That is probably wise," Myrica said. "For now, whenever you do have to do something together, it would be better to include someone else."

"Mostly, he is still just teaching me Whitespeak,

and we can do that around you. You could also learn," Awantia offered.

"That would not be a bad idea. Now that I think about it, I am fine with that. As long as I am not actively required to participate, or my own work will suffer.

"But," Myrica added, "I do not think that you and Ned being alone with each other is the real problem. Our men and women spend time together alone, and you will have to go off without an escort when you travel to the other villages to teach them Whitespeak."

"That is true. It was made clear at the High Council meeting that this would be Ned's work, and because Chief Kotori announced that he would select a companion—and since I am the Chief's official choice—there should be no sense of impropriety. Besides, I find it hard to believe that Sakinay was jealous."

"I do not think it has anything to do with jealousy or impropriety. I believe it is more Sakinay's dislike for the Waschini than anything else; he has always had a problem with the White Men—even before they started causing trouble. I think having the two of you traveling about will uncover everyone's true beliefs about forming a brotherhood with the Waschini, just as your interaction uncovered Sakinay's."

Awantia fell quiet for a moment, then said, "It makes sense, and I believe you are right. I never believed that Sakinay had any feelings for me. It is not that he cares if I take a life-walker or not, just that it should not be a Waschini. However, I have faith that the majority of our people will not feel as Sakinay does. But, we will see."

CHAPTER 14

Riggs had no expectations of lasting out his prison sentence. Despite the isolation in the prisons, word did get around, and as soon as the other inmates found out who he was, it wouldn't take long for their form of justice to be handed out. In some ways, he told himself, death would be better than ten years of hard labor in a facility filled with criminals who would delight in taking out their revenge on anyone in authority.

Throughout his journey there, the handcuffs and ankle shackles constantly bit into his skin, and knowing worse was to come, he considered the pain as the start of his training. He dared hope only that death would not be drawn out and would come quickly.

The outer door slammed behind him with a loud clang, and he looked around at the high stone walls that loomed overhead. A small patch of blue sky reminded him of all he had lost. He was marched in with the other new prisoners and processed. Along with everyone else, he was then handed drab blue garb, all he would wear for however long he lasted.

Of all the prisons he could have been sent to, this was not the worst, but it was bad enough. In the past, the horrible stories of prison life had exacted no compassion from him. He figured the prisoners deserved whatever they got. Now, he realized the same cold-heartedness with which he had previously regarded those sentenced to these places was being directed at him from others on the outside. He was no longer one of them; he was now one of the condemned.

As he was taken to his cell, Riggs tried to avert his gaze from the current residents. He was afraid of what he would see in their eyes. For now, he had a cell to himself, for which he was grateful. He didn't know how long it would last, and he feared who might be assigned to be his cellmate when the time came.

The metal cell door clanked shut. Riggs was surprised that he found the sound comforting. Yes, it kept him in, but it also kept others out. He sat down on the dirty bunk, clutching the scratchy grey blanket they had given him. A bucket in the corner was for him to relieve himself between the regulated bathroom times. The whole place smelled of sweat and mold and dampness. He scanned the ceiling and walls for cockroaches and was relieved to find none.

The latest batch of prisoners had arrived late, so it was already almost time for lights out. He had not eaten all day, and he heard his stomach grumbling. For some reason, his sister Mary's face came to mind, along with the hearty meals she had cooked for him and her family each night. How much he had taken for granted, but it was too late now. He would, no doubt, never know comfort or peace of mind again. And all because of Grayson Stone Morgan the Third.

Riggs didn't sleep. It was a noisy place with no discipline enforced by the guards. Prisoners called to each other all night, some screaming obscenities, others howling like dogs, so even the peace of sleep was out of reach.

He tried sleeping facing the wall, thinking it might give him some privacy, but even though there was no one in the cell with him, he felt exposed and unguarded. So he turned and faced outward, his only view the grey stone walls and the underside of the stripped-down, empty bunk above him. The place was small enough for one person; he couldn't imagine two in there.

The next morning the prisoners were marched to the dining room. The food was dismal, greasy, and unappealing. Everyone got the same amount, and he could see several of the other prisoners eyeing his plate. He kept his head down and shoveled it in, barely chewing so he didn't have to taste it. If it would quell his hunger, then that would have to be good enough.

Many sets of eyes followed Riggs wherever he went. He didn't know how he was supposed to act to keep himself from becoming more of a target. Should he behave like the unaffected tough man or keep to himself as he had been doing?

After breakfast, he was sent to the shoe factory. At first, he was relieved when he heard where he was going. Other prisons were places of hard labor, but this one was not so bad. It would not be pleasant by any means, but at least he wouldn't be an aching mess of muscle strain and blisters at the end of each day.

However, when they went through the double doors, the heat hit Riggs like a blast furnace. It was unbearable, and the smell of leather almost smothered him. There was no ventilation, just high walls with closed windows so dirty that barely any light got in, and certainly no fresh air.

The guard led him to a workstation and told him to sit down until someone came along to show him what to do, so, like everyone else there, he sat down on an uncomfortable wooden stool.

While he was waiting, a big burly man came walking past and bumped into him hard, knocking him off the stool. Riggs hit the floor and scrambled to get back up. The man laughed at him, showing a mouth full of rotting teeth. "I know who you are. We all do. If I were you, I'd watch my back—not that it will help for long." He laughed again.

Riggs wondered how many of the men here he'd

had a hand in putting away. He had no means of knowing, but they knew. But no matter whether they had a personal grudge against him or just a general one because of who he had been, he knew he had no ally and no hope of ever finding one. He was a marked man. It was indeed just a question of time.

A few days passed. So far, the harassment had only involved shoving or being pushed down and kicked, but it was escalating. He was out in the exercise yard trying to mind his own business when one of the guards approached and told him to come along.

He had no illusions about the level of corruption in the prisons. This guard would as likely be an enemy as anyone else. Maybe not a personal one, but favors are favors, and even the guards could be bought.

Riggs followed the uniformed man out of the exercise yard and down a long dank hallway he had not seen before. The further it went, the darker it got, and Riggs started to get a sick feeling in his stomach. He didn't dare ask, and he knew it wouldn't have made any difference; he was powerless to stop whatever was about to happen.

Although not a religious man, he found himself praying anyway. *Just make it swift, please.* He thought again of his sister Mary and was glad he had told her he was going out west and would likely never be back. Maybe, if he were lucky, she would never hear what had become of him. He knew it was a long shot, but he could hope.

The guard stopped and motioned for him to go through an open doorway. As he did so, he saw the guard smirk as if he knew some secret. One Riggs was shortly to learn about for himself.

"Sit down," a voice said from the shadows.

Riggs looked around and found an old barrel to sit on.

"I know who you are."

"Then you have me at a disadvantage," Riggs answered, surprised at his bravado.

"Everyone in here is just itching to do you in, you know. I could make a fortune raffling off who gets the pleasure," the voice continued.

"I suppose business is business everywhere," Riggs quipped. Part of him was wondering at his own audacity. Was he unconsciously trying to provoke this shadow man in order to get it over with?

"Word in here isn't always reliable, so tell me why you are here. A man like yourself doesn't usually make a bad enough mistake to end up here. Or at least, he should know better than to do so."

"I tried blackmailing someone. I let my emotions get the better of me; I wanted revenge, and it backfired."

"And who was this person you were trying to blackmail?"

"A wealthy young man, heir to the Morgan

fortune. Don't know if you have ever heard of the Morgan horse farm—Shadow Ridge?"

"Heard of it."

"He and I had several run-ins. His grandmother and her new husband were supposedly killed. Turned out that didn't happen, and he went up for trial for murdering them. He got off, however."

"So what was that to you?"

"It's a long story," Riggs said.

"We got nothin' but time here," the voice answered.

"The Morgans were rich, very rich. This fellow was the grandson of the old woman who owned the ranch. Her first husband had died years ago, but she continued to run the place with the help of the ranch hands and the stable master, who knew all about horse breeding. This grandson had supposedly been killed long ago with his mother and father, but he turned up years later, alive, and ended up inheriting almost the whole thing."

"So the grandmother was murdered, but he got off?"

"Oh, it is far more interesting than that." Riggs suddenly felt brave. "What do I get for entertaining you with this story?"

"Just go on, and we'll talk about that later. So how does the grandson end up in a trial for their murders if a horse kicked them to death?"

The hair on the back of Riggs' neck stood up. He

had not mentioned that they'd been kicked to death by a horse. Oh, it was the story, but he had not said it.

"Well, through a series of events, the authorities got wind of a rumor that the grandmother and her husband were not dead, that the graves were empty. At least, that they were empty of bodies. They dug up the graves, and it turned out the rumor was true."

Riggs waited for a comment, but there was nothing, so he continued. "One thing led to another. Evidence of foul play pointed to the grandson, and he was arrested and tried for their murders."

"But he got off because of not enough evidence?"

"No. He got off because the grandmother and her husband were still alive."

Suddenly a figure darted out of the shadows and grabbed Riggs by the throat. Riggs stared into eyes filled with rage.

"What did you say? They aren't dead?"

Unable to respond, Riggs raised his hands to try to break the man's grasp on his throat.

The man released him, and he coughed and gasped for a moment.

"What do you mean they aren't dead?"

He looked up at the man who was glaring at him. He had a scruff of red hair, so closely shaven to be barely noticeable. The only other noteworthy thing about him was the blue eyes, though their color was not as intense as those of Grayson Morgan.

"Give me a minute," Riggs said, wracking his memory in an attempt to figure out who this could be, who would be so upset at this news. Finally, he got it.

"You must be Louis Morgan." Riggs looked him up and down. If the person standing over him had ever been a man of refinement, no one could ever have told. Whatever social mannerisms he had once embodied were long gone, replaced with a brusqueness laced with aggression. No longer recognizable as a man of sophistication, there was only a hulking brute.

"Yeah. I am. Or I was. And you had better finish the story quickly because I am not a patient man. So my mother, Vivian Morgan, is not dead?"

"No. It was all a ruse. Something she said she wanted so she could move away and start a new life."

"You saw her? At the trial?"

"No. She sent a letter. It was legitimate—convinced the judge, at least."

The man stepped back a few feet, obviously still in shock over the news and trying to process it.

"What happened to Shadow Ridge?"

"Your mother left it to a woman named Mrs. Thomas. She and her sons are running it now."

"Leave it to my mother to do something like that. Marry the damn farm hand and leave a fortune to the housekeeper. She never did understand her station in life."

"I remember your case. You were sentenced to life in prison for setting up the murders of your brother and sister-in-law and trying to kill your nephew."

"You know where he is?" Louis asked.

"Your nephew? Grayson Morgan? Yes, I do. Well, thereabouts."

"You can tell me where to find him?"

Riggs almost laughed, then stopped himself. "You are in here for life."

"Well, that is a matter of opinion. I got out once, and I can get out again if I want; I just haven't had any reason to. Until now."

"No, I can't tell you where to find him. I would have to take you there. It's out in the locals' territory."

The man stepped back partly into the shadows and leaned back against some shelves, his hand running over his chin as he eyed Riggs.

After a moment of silence, he said, "So this is the deal. I will give you my protection, make sure no one kills you until we can escape. Then, when we get out, you will take me to where that sniveling nephew of mine is. After that, you can do what you will."

"Do you want to try to find your mother? Because no one knows where she is."

"No. I stopped caring about her when she stood by and let me get locked up in here and then left everything to that savage."

Riggs was taken aback by Louis' use of the word. At least they had that in common, hatred of Grayson Stone Morgan the Third.

He feared he might be pushing his luck, but at

the moment, he had something Louis Morgan wanted. Information. "Not meaning to sound ungrateful, but if I break out with you, we'll both just end up back here, or worse,"

"You do what I tell you. Exactly as I tell you, and you'll be out in five, maybe seven years. If I can wait that long, then that's when I'll make my break. Otherwise, when I say it's time, it's time. At least you'll be alive if I tell the others to leave you alone."

Riggs thought for a moment and realized he had no choice but to take the deal. He had heard of inmates who somehow climbed to a position of power within the prison and had ways of getting what they wanted, but what was behind Louis' position of influence, he could not begin to guess. It was just a bonus for him that they shared a desire for revenge against the same man.

After that encounter, things got easier for Riggs. He got a better job, not in the smothering heat of the cobbler shop, but working in the kitchen cleaning and preparing the food. He still felt eyes following him and knew that if anything happened to Louis Morgan, his own time there would quickly end. Whatever hold Louis had over the rest of the inmates, it was the only thing keeping him alive.

Moart'Tor and Naha's relationship was an amiable one as she was easygoing and did not demand much of him. She had decorated their living space with the usual materials available and made meals for him every day. He had no complaints, though there was no real spark between them.

As the days went on, he began to think more and more about Kayerm and his time there. He regretted he had not realized sooner that the Sassen and the Akassa were not the horrors his father claimed them to be. He was also sorry he had not stayed longer after having that change of heart. He realized his ingratitude after so many had left wherever they were living to return to Kayerm for his benefit. And, though he tried not to, he often thought of Eitel and wondered what had become of her. He was sure she would eventually pair, as he had, but that made him sad, so she was one part of his experience there that he tried to push out of his mind.

One day, he was particularly troubled and unable to stop thinking of her no matter how hard he tried, so he sought out Pan. Now that time had passed, he felt, in retrospect, that he had rushed into pairing. He had wanted to keep moving forward, and though Naha was a good mate, he wished he had held out for someone who made his heart sing as Eitel had.

"Is there anything you can tell me about what happened after you brought me here?" he started with. "To those at Kayerm?"

"Just that they returned to their homes. Is there something specific you want to know, Moart'Tor?"

"The female, Eitel. She was kind to me, and I

rebuked her. I think of her often and wonder how she is doing."

"I will return someday, and you are welcome to go with me if you would like. I think you should see Kthama in person, as well as the adjoining system where the Sassen live."

"They do not all live together?" he asked. When he had watched part of the High Council assembly with Pan, both Akassa and Sassen had been present.

"There are separate systems. It is a long story of how the Sassen left Kayerm and came to live at what was known as Kthama Minor, now Kht'shWea. Would you like to hear it?"

Pan spent much of the afternoon telling Moart'Tor the history of their people, from the time when the rebels left Kayerm and went out on their own to the opening of Kthama Minor and the creation of the twelve white Sassen Guardians.

He was overcome at learning of the twelve Guardians. "The Great Spirit moves mightily on behalf of the Akassa and the Sassen," he remarked after hearing all of it.

Pan had no qualms about Moart'Tor's intentions, so she also told him that the Promised One had been born and that in a few years, she would bring him to Lulnomia to start his training.

"The Promised One is an Akassa?" he was stupefied. "That is even more proof they are not mistakes to be corrected. If only my family at Zuenerth knew of this. Faced with such evidence, how could they continue to believe as my father has poisoned their minds to do."

"It has always been my hope to reunite the rebel Mothoc with us here at Lulnomia. Perhaps it will still happen, and you may well be a part of that, Moart'-Tor. Only time will tell, but we must be open to all possibilities of reaching them. The Great Spirit's will is for unity, not division."

Then she changed the subject to something she had been meaning to ask him for some time. "Are you still happy here?"

"Happy enough. Naha is a good mate, but I cannot help but wish my mother and my siblings were here."

"What of your father? Kaisak?"

"Yes, there are others, of course, not just my mother and brothers. My father. Your brother, Dak'-Tor, and his family. Oh, I suppose all of them. But I particularly miss my mother."

"What is she like?"

"Strong, Feisty. Proud. She has a fire in her that sometimes she cannot control. She and my father have argued terribly on and off, so it has been a tumultuous union. But she loves us deeply and would sacrifice her own life for any of us. Even though I was seeded by your brother and not her mate, she never let me feel left out or different."

"And did Kaisak?"

"Hmmm. Now that I am reflecting, I think he

thought differently of me, but I only see it in retrospect."

Through all the centuries, Pan had never visited the rebel camp, though she could have, just as she had visited other places. No one would have known, and she could have watched her brother and his family and learned how he was faring. But there had always been a check in her spirit that kept her from finding out. Now, whatever had been holding her back was lifting.

"Tell me about my brother. Does he believe what Kaisak does?"

"If he does not, he has never spoken against it. Though Kaisak is the Adik'Tar, your brother is a Leader in his own right. There is somewhat of a division within the group, though it is not evidenced by open conflict; it is just that Dak'Tor has his—followers is perhaps the best word. He has seeded many offling on the Leader's orders, but he is actively father only to a handful. The rest are like I was, knowing he had seeded me but having a different male as their father. His mate is called Iria. She is beautiful, dark-coated. One of their offling has the same grey eyes as you. Many suspect her of being some type of Guardian because of her eyes."

Pan listened as Moart'Tor continued telling her about Dak'Tor and life at Zuenerth. There was no mention of the crystal, and she was not going to ask. Was it possible that in all this time, Dak'Tor had never revealed its existence? If so, what did that mean? Was his alliance perhaps, in truth, not with Kaisak? And what of the crystal? Her mother had told her An'Kru would need it when he freed Moc'Tor from the vortex. Would An'Kru himself retrieve the crystal when he was ready to use it, or would it fall to her to retrieve it before that time?

Pan had searched for direction but had never received any. Whatever the fate of the crystal, it was not yet given to her to play a role in its recovery. She suspected that Wrollonan'Tor knew what had become of it, but he had refused to answer her questions, simply directing her back to her own guidance for the answer.

Dak'Tor had never told anyone but his mate, Iria, about the crystal, and only so that if something happened to him, she would know to give it to Pan when the Guardian returned. It was tucked safely in an upper cavity in their living quarters. Most living areas had such a storage shaft dug back into one of the walls for items that needed to be out of any offling's reach, but Dak'Tor had made a second, unexpected space with an opening so expertly crafted that no one would ever see the plug which sealed it.

There the crystal remained, carefully wrapped and waiting for destiny to call.

CHAPTER 15

Khon'Tor had taken Urilla Wuti's counsel to heart. He took long walks outside the Far High Hills, sometimes with Tehya but mostly on his own, each time spent trying to determine his true motives in wanting to confess his crime against Adia. When he was alone, he spoke out loud to the Great Spirit, asking for guidance. The last thing he wanted was to make matters worse for those he had harmed, but what he could not come to peace with was the shame borne by Acaraho and Adia. The People had forgiven them and accepted them both, and the past seemed to have no active bearing on Acaraho's leadership of the High Rocks. But that did not negate the mantle of shame that had been placed on them and was not theirs to bear.

"I believe it is time," he told Tehya, "No matter how much I try to shake it, to convince myself that it is in the past and everyone has moved on, it still grieves my soul that the People think Adia and Acaraho broke her Healer's vow never to mate or bear offspring and that Nimida does not have her rightful place as Adia's daughter."

"I am prepared for this, my love. I have known all along that this day might come." As they stood together, she ran her hand lovingly up and down his muscled arm. "We will be fine. My only hope is for our offspring—that when they learn the truth, we can somehow ensure they will not be badly affected."

He looked down into the beautiful amber eyes that were so full of love for him. "I wish I could set this aside, but I cannot. However, first I need to speak with Adia, Nimida, and Nootau.

"I cannot ask you to be less than you are. The fact that you feel such a burden in your soul to set this straight proves even more how much you have changed. I will pray for mercy and forgiveness and that those who learn this truth will humbly consider their own failings before they pass harsh judgment on you."

Khon'Tor did not want Tehya to come with him, but she insisted. "No, I will not let you face this alone. They need to see that I know you did this and that I still stand with you."

"Then we need to go to Kthama."

Acaraho was surprised to see Khon'Tor, Tehya, and Urilla Wuti—who had insisted on participating in her position as Overseer. There had been no word sent regarding their coming. But Adia immediately knew why they had come, and her heart grew heavy for what was about to take place. She and Acaraho accompanied Khon'Tor and Tehya to the living quarters they always used when they were at the High Rocks.

"I know why you are here, Khon'Tor," she said as they all stood outside the door. "You are going to tell the People of the High Rocks about the past. About Nimida and Nootau."

"I want to," Khon'Tor said, "but only if they both agree. It is the truth, and no matter how ugly the truth is, I believe that when you speak it, you are standing in the presence of the Great Spirit."

"I do not know what to say to either of you," Acaraho said. "Your bravery is beyond measure. I speak for both of us, Khon'Tor, when I say you do not need to do this. It is in the past, and its effects have long since dissipated. I question the benefit of confessing this now."

"The truth needs to come to light," Khon'Tor said. "I believe you both when you say you do not need me to do this, and before I do, I want to talk to both Nootau and Nimida. I am afraid that until the truth is known, some part of them is locked away from themselves. I cannot explain it fully, only that I believe this to be true. They have a right to their true heritage being known, and Nimida needs to be able to claim Adia as her mother. You and Adia have a right for the record to be set straight."

"I can see we cannot change your mind. When would you like me to assemble the People?"

"If Nootau and Nimida agree it is the right thing to do, then perhaps tomorrow morning."

"If you wish to wait, we will look for them both and bring them here to see you," Adia offered.

"Thank you. Has Oh'Dar returned from Wilde Edge?"

"Yes, and we will prepare him. Do you want his grandparents to attend?" Acaraho asked.

"Oh'Dar's grandmother is still faithfully writing our people's history, I believe," Khon'Tor answered. "This is part of that; she also needs to hear it."

Nimida and Nootau had been brought to Khon'Tor and Tehya's quarters and were waiting to hear what the meeting was about.

Khon'Tor walked a few steps, as was his habit when about to speak, while Tehya remained seated.

"I need to talk to you before I make a final decision because what I am planning to do affects you both.

"I believe it is time for the truth to come out about what I did to your mother and that it resulted in your births. I want to clear her name and Acaraho's because they have lived with a shadow of shame cast over them that they did not and do not deserve. And it also impacted your lives. If I confess what I did, it will clear the record for them, and it will make your true heritage known, so you, Nimida, can take your rightful place as Adia's daughter, and you and Nootau can openly claim each other as siblings."

"I do not know what to say." Nimida turned to her brother.

"There will be repercussions," Nootau said.

"But not against any of you," Khon'Tor replied. "I fully expect an outpouring of support for the four of you, which is as it should be."

"What about you, Tehya?" Nimida looked across at her.

"I support my mate. If in his heart he feels it is time for this to come out, then I will publicly stand by him and support him. But, first, he wants to make sure that you are both aware of his intention and that you will be helped and not in any way damaged or inconvenienced if he goes through with it.

"I do pray, however," she added, "that they realize he is not the same person who committed this terrible crime."

"It would relieve a burden," Nimida said. "And I think I am ready to take my place as Adia's daughter." She smiled at Nootau. "And as your sister."

Nootau finally nodded. "My mother and father both know you want to do this, right?"

"Yes, that is why they brought you here. I met with them first."

"There is no easy answer," Nootau said. "It is difficult to live with a lie, but it can also be difficult to live with the truth. But all in all, if you are willing to do it, I also believe it is right to set the record straight."

That evening, Adia and Acaraho took Oh'Dar aside to speak with him privately.

Adia began. "My son, tomorrow, a major revelation is going to take place, one that has the potential to unnerve the entire community. We wanted you to know about it before it is revealed to everyone else."

Puzzled, Oh'Dar looked first at his mother and then at his father.

Adia explained that Khon'Tor was coming to Kthama to confess a crime he had committed long ago. When she told him what Khon'Tor had done, Oh'Dar flew to his feet.

"He took you Without Your Consent? A Healer?"

"Yes, and I kept it from everyone, for everyone's sake," Adia explained. "I pray you will understand why."

"I understand that he got away with one of the greatest wrongs that can be committed. Why would you protect him by keeping it secret?" Oh'Dar's face was twisted with anger and bewilderment.

Acaraho jumped in. "If the community had

known what he did, it would have torn itself apart. Not just those of us at the High Rocks, but everyone. Word would have spread far and wide, and while some would have believed your mother, others would have said she was lying, so lines would have been drawn, and families split apart. Her intent was to minimize the damage, which had to be at her own expense."

"And tomorrow, everyone else is going to find this out?" he asked, now shifting agitatedly back and forth on his feet.

"Not everyone else. Nootau knows already, and so does Nimida," Adia said.

"Why Nimida?"

Adia then told Oh'Dar the entire story. He asked many questions about why Nimida was sent away and when Nootau had found out. His parents did their best to answer each one as candidly as they could, and then all three sat together in silence for some time.

Later, Adia asked Mapiya to come to the next day's assembly to support Nimida. The older female's interest was piqued when she realized it had something to do with her much-loved adopted daughter.

In another area of Kthama, Nootau was telling his mate he needed to speak to her.

Iella listened patiently until he had finished. "Nimida is your sister? With all these years of not knowing, I cannot imagine what you must both now be going through. And it is all going to be revealed in the morning? Tomorrow and the days ahead will no doubt be especially hard on everyone involved. Is there anything I can do to help you?"

An air of excitement was rolling through the High Rocks as word spread that there would be an assembly directly following first meal, but only the adults were to be in attendance.

Many were already gathered in the Great Chamber even before the announcement horn sounded. At the front of the room, Khon'Tor waited with Tehya, Acaraho, Adia, and Urilla Wuti. Acaraho held the 'Tor Leader's Staff, a signal that something very important was about to take place.

Oh'Dar and his grandparents with Acise, Iella, and Nootau sat near the front. On the other side of Nootau sat Nimida and Tar with Mapiya. Khon'Tor knew Adia had asked that they all sit together, though they probably would have anyway.

There were so many familiar faces, and Khon'Tor looked from one to another. He saw anticipation, curiosity, and some nervousness and wondered what he would see when he was finished doing what he had come here to do.

Acaraho stepped to the center and slammed the Leader's staff on the floor, the custom when beginning a meeting of great importance. Those who were talking immediately fell silent.

"Khon'Tor, who led the People of the High Rocks for centuries before I took over leadership, has asked to address you. I have no preamble other than to ask you to give him the respect and consideration that is his due; his record of leadership stands on its own merits.

"Neither Adia nor I asked Khon'Tor to come here to do what he is about to do, but it is his choice, and we respect his right to decide what he feels is the best course of action, no matter how difficult."

The People exchanged glances, and small, speculative murmurings started.

Nimida looked nervously at Nootau, sitting to her left. "This is going to change everything," she whispered.

"I know."

As Acaraho moved to the side, Khon'Tor stepped forward. Tehya took a step, too, and he glanced around to see her standing slightly behind him and to one side.

"When my father passed the leadership of the High Rocks to me," he began, "I knew it was a tremendous responsibility. I vowed to follow in his footsteps, to be the type of Leader the People could look up to and trust. I vowed to inspire you with faith in my abilities and my good will so that no one should doubt that the decisions I made were for the good of all at Kthama and not in any way self-serving. For many years, I believe I lived up to that standard I set for myself. And then I made a terrible mistake, one that only a few of you know about. But now it is time for all of you to hear the truth about the heinous crime I committed against one of our own. Against one who did not in any way deserve or provoke what I did to her, and who, to her credit, has kept the secret of my crime all this time in order to protect the community she loves and has served so faithfully."

Not a breath could be heard.

"I am not here to excuse what I did because there is no excuse for it. I am here to set the record straight so that, hopefully, some of the damage and pain I inflicted will be eased. That is my prayer, at least. I do not ask for your forgiveness, or your understanding, as I deserve neither. What I do ask is that you listen carefully and do not in any way believe that what I did was anything less than what it was. A grievous sin against one who did not deserve it or the suffering that ensued."

Khon'Tor looked back at Tehya and was shored up by the love he saw in her eyes.

"All these years, you have believed that Acaraho fathered Nootau. That he and the Healer Adia had together broken her vow of celibacy. And though you forgave them, the fact remains that this is what you have believed all this time. But it is not true."

Khon'Tor could almost feel the wave of confusion roll through the crowd. Some people glanced at each other, brows raised and mouths open. Others sat transfixed, waiting for him to continue.

"I am the father of Nootau. I seeded him and his twin sister, whom you know as Nimida. I took the Healer Without Consent, and she and Acaraho bore the shame that should have been mine."

Some in the crowd were stunned into silence, but many broke out into chatter. They quietened once more when Khon'Tor started speaking again. He had only guessed at what he might expect, but this was not it.

"The history is long and complicated. Adia bore not just one offspring but two, and I was not aware of Nimida's birth. She was sent away to be raised elsewhere, to protect her from me, in case, in my wrath against Adia, she might also suffer. Only later, when Nootau was to be paired, did I learn about Nimida's existence. The High Council had selected her to pair with Nootau, and Adia could not allow that to happen. The crux of it is, of course, that they were not paired, and the High Council members learned what I had done.

"You are wondering why I was not punished at that time. The High Council wanted to banish me for my crime, but Adia stood up to them and did not allow it. Again, her sacrifice was to prevent the destruction of our community at the High Rocks and those elsewhere. She exemplified the second law, that the needs of the community come before the needs of the individual. She deserved justice to be served, but she forfeited it on your behalf.

"Nothing can right the wrong I committed, but

now, with time having passed, I have brought you the truth. I wish to rectify the undeserved shame that Adia and Acaraho have had to live with and to acknowledge Nimida and Nootau's rightful heritage."

In the silence, Urilla Wuti stepped forward, "I know this is a shock. I know it will take time for you to take in what you have just heard. But I ask that you keep this within the walls of Kthama. This is not something Khon'Tor has asked. This is something I am asking for the sake of Nimida and Nootau and their future offspring, who should not have to pay for the sins of those in the past. And now, please give them both their privacy. None of us can fully understand what this recent revelation has been like for them."

Tehya moved closer to Khon'Tor and took his hand as he made way for Acaraho to step forward and speak.

"Please, go back to your lives and make peace with this however you can. It is far in the past and has no bearing on our lives today, other than it is a truth that Khon'Tor deeply felt needed to be made known for Adia's sake and mine as well as for Nootau and Nimida."

Throughout Khon'Tor's speech, Adia had been watching Nimida and Nootau. She had felt the emotions, the brief spell of relief, and now, awkward self-consciousness. She now saw Nimida reach out to grasp Mapiya's hand and lean in to accept her embrace. As Nootau looked across at Acaraho, she could feel her son's deep sadness. His truth had been both given and taken away. Khon'Tor's confession gave him his true birthright, but it cost him the universal belief that Acaraho was his father by blood. Nootau was still of the House of 'Tor, but not the son of the one they all believed him to be. The sorrow that filled him was almost unbearable to Adia, and she fought back the tears of her grief for him.

"Wait," Nootau rose to his feet. "Please, I also need to say something." He walked up to the front.

Every eye in the room followed him, and Adia took a deep breath to steady her emotions.

"All my life, I grew up believing Acaraho was my father. It was only recently that I learned otherwise. Since then, my emotions have been in turmoil. I have had to redefine what fatherhood means. Yes, Khon'Tor is my blood father. He seeded me, no matter the circumstances; that is the truth. But it was Acaraho who raised me and taught me right from wrong. He taught me how to hunt, fish, and follow the patterns of the stars, how to be a good citizen of the High Rocks and how to be a good mate to a female. He encouraged me, shared my triumphs, and consoled me in my failures. In every way that matters, Acaraho is my father and always will be."

Adia's heart ached as she felt Acaraho reach deep to try to suppress his reaction but could not.

He looked at Nootau, who immediately fell into his father's arms. "My son, my son," Acaraho said.

"Always and forever, I am your son," Nootau replied.

They clung to each other for a moment, and Adia felt the shock, astonishment, and other emotions that had held the crowd captive shifting into something else. Compassion filled the room—not from every soul but from the majority, and with it came a small sense of the suffering that those before them had endured.

She walked to the front and wrapped her arms around her mate and her son. Then she looked into the crowd and extended her hand to Nimida, who accepted the invitation and joined their circle. As her daughter did so, Adia looked up to see Urilla Wuti step forward and raise her arm for attention.

"Please, as Acaraho has asked, go back to your lives. Whatever you decide about this, I want you to understand there are levels within this story that you will never know and that most people could probably not understand. Adia fought the High Council to save this community from self-destruction, recognizing the huge challenges that lay ahead for us and fearing we were not all strong enough to realize that Leaders are flawed. That they are little different from the rest of us, although their mistakes have further-reaching effects because of their station and influence. Khon'Tor was later severely punished for his crime, and no one forced him to come here and tell us this. Tehya insisted on being present to stand with him, and like her, those of us who have known Khon'Tor for many years can attest that he is no longer the person who committed this grievous crime.

"But, in time, if you have not already, you will each, in your own hearts, judge Khon'Tor. It is our nature. But I ask that in your judging, you seek humility. Ask yourself, if your greatest sin were revealed, what would you hope for from those around you? And I am confident that the answer is mercy, at least, if forgiveness is too far out of reach. Adia and Acaraho have long ago forgiven him, and as for Nootau and Nimida, only they can speak of their own journey through this.

"As your Overseer, I leave you with one last thing, and that is to request that you not share this information beyond our walls here. Everyone involved has asked for privacy. What is done is done; please leave them to heal their wounds and discover where their paths will now lead them. Let this be an act of healing for all of us."

The People slowly rose to their feet and began filing out. Adia approached the front, and while gently touching Khon'Tor's hand, placed her arm around little Tehya. Acaraho then walked over to her, still holding the Leader's staff, and in the People's gesture of brotherhood, he placed a hand on Khon'-Tor's shoulder. The two locked gazes.

Both were Adia and Acaraho's gifts to Khon'Tor, a

public display of the forgiveness Urilla Wuti had just spoken of.

Mapiya turned to Nimida, who had rejoined her and Tar. “Oh, my poor dear; I am so sorry. So this is what has been troubling you so much lately.”

“Yes,” Nimida answered, “and though I could not tell you, I am glad you know now.”

Nimida turned to look at Acaraho and the others still at the front. “Look at them. They have found peace, and if they can, perhaps I can too. I know I do not want to live with any animosity and resentment in my heart. The Overseer is right; what is done is done. Living in anger will only rob me of finding happiness in my life. Oh, Mapiya, please pray for me; pray that I may continue to find my own peace.”

“I will, I promise I will,” Mapiya answered. “And Nootau will help you; I know it.”

When the chamber was almost empty, Nimida went back up to her mother, who was still with Acaraho and the Overseer. Tar followed closely behind her.

“Khon’Tor did not have to do that,” she said.

Urilla Wuti turned to her. “There is a balance to everything. Light and dark, good and bad. Rarely in this realm is there complete polarization at one end or another, and good things can come out of terrible mistakes.”

"I am learning that, Overseer. Just as I am learning how toxic unforgiveness is. And I appreciate your plea for discretion," Nimida continued. "We hope to have offspring someday, and we will have to figure out what we are going to tell them, which is making me realize the conflict of this situation from the other point of view."

She turned to look at Tar, who stood next to her, his jaw hard set. "My intention is to go forward with my mate."

"Iella and I will move forward with you," Nootau said, putting his arm around his sister's shoulders.

"We have had years to come to grips with this, but I wonder what will happen now," Adia mused.

"Each will react according to his or her nature, as is the way of things," Urilla Wuti said. "Those who have a modicum of humility will tread lightly toward condemnation. Others who have a strong sense of compassion may more quickly see the complexity of the situation. Those who have a strict idea of what constitutes justice may feel Khon'Tor was never satisfactorily brought to task for his misdeeds, and they may harbor resentment for some time. But it is not his singular act that they must wrestle with, Adia; it is the years that he let you and Acaraho bear the shame that should have been his."

Once they were out of earshot, Tar stopped walking and said to his mate, "Khon'Tor; I have known him all my life. How can it be? My sister gave her life for his and Acaraho's. She believed in him, in his greatness. And now this."

Then his attitude shifted as he looked at Nimida, "And yet, without his crime, you would not exist, and we would not be together. I love you with all my heart, which is all that really matters. Tell me how to help you through this whole situation."

"Just be with me. Now that he has confessed, I am not sure how I feel. Some relief, of course, and still some anger, but also, strangely, some guilt that everyone now thinks less of him."

"That is his fault, not yours," Tar reminded her.

"I know, and yet I still feel a little sorry for him. And for Tehya."

Tar pulled her close, "That is your kind heart. And it is a lot to assimilate because things have been happening very quickly. You do not have to figure it all out at once. It will take time, as the Overseer said, and that is one thing you have. And you also have all my support."

"Oh, my," Miss Vivian said when it was over. "Oh, my, I don't know what to say."

Oh'Dar was also still struggling with it; even though he had known in advance what was going to happen, it had taken him all night simply to start coming to grips with it. All this time and none of them had known. Nootau himself had only just found out. Nimida as well.

It explained the incongruity that, to him, had always hung over what everyone thought to be true. He, like some others, had found it hard to believe that Adia would abandon her Healer's vows or that Acaraho would participate.

Most people assumed that passion had overtaken their better judgment, and over time, had forgiven them their indiscretion. Oh'Dar hoped that in the same way, the community would eventually come to forgive Khon'Tor. Not for Khon'Tor's sake, but for those of his brother and Nimida—who was now his sister.

"In the end," Ben said, "they are all only people. Just like us."

Oh'Dar thought it was the perfect summary and recognition that though they were from different races, they were ultimately the same in their challenges, triumphs, and failures.

"I do not want to record this in the history of the People, but I know I must," Miss Vivian said. "I had hopes that in time, I'Layah would take over this responsibility, yet knowing she would at some point read about all of this has me questioning my thinking."

"By the time she needs to step in, Grandmother," Oh'Dar said, "she will be old enough to understand."

"Oh, dear, Grayson, I fear you do not realize how old Ben and I truly are."

"Please don't talk like that. You have many years left, and I can't bear the thought of being without you."

"Your grandmother is right, son," Ben chimed in. "We do not have unlimited time here. Others will have to take over the school, and yet others help Bidzel and Yuma'qia in trying to solve the breeding problem even though, honestly, I do not see a solution—but a new set of eyes might see something we have missed."

"Are you thinking of Ned?" Oh'Dar asked.

"Yes; he has studied animal science, which no doubt includes something about breeding, and he has a technical mind. He is the logical choice, and we are lucky that he decided to come here to live."

CHAPTER 16

Khon'Tor and Tehya had already explained that they planned on leaving before first light. Tehya was anxious to get home to their offspring and hoped to establish for her family as much normalcy as possible.

So, very early the next morning, they made their way down the dimly lit tunnels toward the Mother Stream, as it was less likely to disturb others than leaving through the Great Entrance. As they rounded a corner, a large male suddenly stepped in front of them, brandishing a blade and blocking the way.

Khon'Tor instinctively pushed Tehya behind him and extended his arms to shield her further. He couldn't see who the male was because he was wearing a hood. Then a jolt of recognition went through him.

"Why so shocked, Adik'Tar; did you think you would go unpunished for what you did?"

With the knife extended, he slashed quickly to the side, and Khon'Tor moved with him, always keeping himself between Tehya and the attacker.

"Oh, wait. The hood; is it familiar to you? I suspected it might be yours, but now I can see it is. You made a serious mistake; you should not have buried it in that patch of ginseng. So, tell me, what crimes does this hood represent?"

Khon'Tor's thoughts were racing. The assailant was disguising his voice, which meant that perhaps he might be familiar. But, regardless, he had found the hood, now long forgotten, used to rape Linoi, the Overseer's niece. Khon'Tor's past crimes were rising up again to take their toll on him, but his only thought was for his precious mate.

In the next moment, the stranger made another move. Still in front of Tehya, Khon'Tor stood ready. As the attacker drove the blade forward, Khon'Tor caught him square under the chin with an uppercut, sending him sprawling back, but not before the blade had found its target.

Khon'Tor doubled over as the blade entered his side, but his only thought was still to protect Tehya. He heard her screaming in the background and saw the other male stumble to his feet and run off. Once the attacker was out of sight, he let himself fall to the ground, his hand instinctively going to the blade that was protruding from his side.

Tehya dropped down next to her fallen mate, hysterically screaming. She didn't know what to do; she should get help, and yet she didn't want to leave his side in case the attacker returned. She knew not to remove the blade, as it would only make the wound bleed more furiously.

Khon'Tor had one hand wrapped around the handle.

"No, no!" she screamed at him. "Do not pull it out!" She was terrified he might be in shock and not thinking clearly, so she placed her hand over his, hoping to keep him from dislodging the blade.

Though it was early, her screams had been heard, and within a moment, several people came running to their aid. One of them was Nootau, who immediately told someone to run and tell the Healer and then to find Acaraho or anyone else in authority.

Tehya spoke soothingly to her mate, telling him to hold on, that help was coming. After what seemed like forever, Adia, Acaraho, Iella, and several large males arrived to bring aid. Adia carefully examined the wound, from which the blade still protruded. She knew that at some point, it would have to be removed, but not until absolutely necessary.

While the Healer attended to Khon'Tor, Acaraho asked Tehya what had happened, and then Acaraho quickly barked out an order to one of the males to run and find as many guards as he could and begin searching for anyone outside Kthama or near the entrance and detain whoever they found. Then he ran down the tunnel in the direction the attacker had gone.

Iella had brought as many clean woven cloths as she could find, and Tehya kept talking to her mate, telling him how much she loved him, how much she and their offspring needed him, and to hold on. The fact that he was still conscious was a good sign, as shock was a real possibility and would reduce his chances of surviving.

Adia kept pressure on the wound, praying that the bleeding would slow. From what she could tell from the amount of blood, it had not pierced anything critical, but the proof would be when she pulled the blade out. She was worried about his temperature as he was lying on the cold floor but didn't want to move him until absolutely necessary. Eventually, the bleeding slowed, but still not wanting to remove the blade, she asked the males to carefully move him to the Healer's Quarters, where she would have more light and everything she needed close at hand.

Then Adia called for her son's attention. "Nootau. When they lift him up, keep pressure on the wound. It is very important. Move along with them and do not let go until I tell you, do you understand?"

"I do."

Khon'Tor moaned as they lifted him, while Tehya, still at his side, tried not to be in the way.

The males slowly carried him, followed by a small procession.

Once Khon'Tor was in the Healer's Quarters and prone, Adia decided it was time to remove the blade. She knew the body's natural response to a serious injury, which had kept him out of too much pain, was now fading. It would hurt more than if she had removed it earlier, but she could not have chanced removing it too early.

The Healer looked at the blade. The handle was slick with blood, and she found a piece of cloth to wrap around it so it wouldn't slip from her grasp.

"Are you ready?" she asked him. Khon'Tor nodded, and Adia pulled the blade out, as close as possible to the angle it had gone in. Iella immediately pushed more clean cloths into the long slit in his side. Both were relieved that the bleeding was not profuse.

Adia set the blade on a side table. "We have to clean the wound, Khon'Tor. I am sorry."

"Do what you have to do. As long as Tehya is alright."

"I am quite alright." Tehya leaned down and gazed into his eyes. "I am right here."

With the wound flushed and packed with clean cloths, there was nothing else to do but administer the Healer's concoction to reduce the chance of infection.

Acaraho returned, clutching a dark hood in one hand. "I found this a way down the tunnel leading to the Mother Stream, but we did not find the assailant."

Then he asked Tehya to tell him what had happened in whatever detail she could.

When she had finished, she glanced at the blade, still partially wrapped in the cloth and lying on the side table, and said, "Khon'Tor did not even step out of the way, Acaraho. He just let the attacker drive the blade into his side. Why?"

"He did not want to take a chance of exposing you. I would have done the same thing."

Then, as her feelings came flooding in, Tehya began to sob. "I never want to see that thing again. I want it out of my sight."

When Adia and Iella had done all they could, Adia stepped out into the hall with Acaraho.

"Since neither of them could see the attacker's face, we will have a hard time figuring out who did this," Acaraho said. "I will place several guards outside with orders that none but the Healers, Tehya, and myself are to enter."

Nootau joined them in the hallway. "I think he is asleep. Tehya does not look as if she will leave his side anytime soon, but she is still upset at having the weapon in the room."

"I will remove it, and then I will send word to

Harak'Sar," Acaraho said, "I am sure whoever is caring for Arismae and Bracht'Tor will have no trouble keeping them for as long as necessary."

"Mama," Nootau said. It was some time since he had called her that. "Do you think he could die?"

"I do not know, son. A blade wound is very dangerous, but it could have been so much worse. If the blade had been more to the center, he would have bled to death by now. It was not gushing blood, so that is a good sign, and the real risk now is infection."

"I would like to help however I can. I can bring food in and make sure the bandages are clean and dry."

Adia was touched that Nootau wanted to help. "Thank you. I am sure Tehya will also appreciate that. We will all do everything we can for him, but the most everyone can do to help is to pray."

While Adia was caring for Khon'Tor, Acaraho was having all the males who were up and around stopped and questioned, even though the attack had taken place on the route to the Mother Stream, and the attacker could easily have left Kthama that way.

Acaraho hand-picked some of his most trusted guards, placing them up and down the passage to the Healer's Quarters. He also made sure Tehya was never alone no matter where she went, though she seldom left her mate.

He couldn't remember a more satisfying feeling than when the blade penetrated Khon'Tor's side. But then Khon'Tor's mate started screaming, so he got away as fast as he could. He bolted down the tunnel toward the Mother Stream before realizing that her screams would have alerted others, and the watchers would be waiting to see if anyone exited to the surface from that route.

He knew the tunnels of the High Rocks well, every twist and turn, shortcut, and circuitous route to get where he wanted. He headed for an intersection because going straight ahead would take him to the Mother Stream. He ran down the tunnel on the left, tossed the hood on the floor, then backtracked and went down the other arm of the tunnel. He snaked his way in and out and finally, unnoticed, entered the Great Chamber, where he unobtrusively walked over to the food servers, picked out food for first meal, and sat down.

His jaw ached from Khon'Tor's punch, but if there was bruising, his beard would cover it, and he didn't taste any blood, so he knew his mouth was undamaged. He was confident there would be no way to identify him.

It did not take long before everyone at the High Rocks was talking about the attack on their former Adik'Tar. Acaraho walked in on one such conversation between a group of guards and watchers.

"No doubt they will never find out who did it," one of the males said.

"It could have been anyone," another added. "Despite what he did to our Healer, I do not condone someone trying to kill him. I am sure it was related."

"I wonder why Acaraho did not kill Khon'Tor over it long ago," the first male added.

"Were you not listening?" said a third. "The Healer did not want that. She put our best interests and the welfare of the High Rocks ahead of her own. I am sure he wanted to, but if he had, it would have gone against everything she was trying to achieve. But I am sure it was hard for him to honor her wishes. It certainly would have been for me."

Acaraho came up behind them. "You are exactly right, Zsorn."

They turned when they heard his voice.

"I did want to kill him," the Leader said. "But out of respect for Adia, I did not. What good would have come of it? It would have satisfied my need for vengeance but, in the end, done more harm than good. Right now, Khon'Tor is fighting for his life, and my hope is that no one is wishing for his death. How many times must it be said that he is not the same person who committed that crime? If Adia can forgive him, how can we be expected to do any less?"

Nimida was coming in from outside and appeared to have overheard the conversation. She approached the group. "May I speak with you, Acaraho?"

He excused himself and stepped away with her.

"I want you to call a meeting, please. I would like to address the People of the High Rocks; I am ready."

"May I ask what you would say?"

"I know you do not want me to make matters worse, and that is not my intention. If anything, I want to try to quell any harsh feelings against Khon'Tor and ask everyone to pray for his recovery."

"I see," Acaraho said. "Very well, then, I will call everyone together this afternoon. He can use all the prayers he can get."

Adia was reluctant to leave Khon'Tor, but knowing he was in Nadiwani's skilled care, she agreed to Nimida's request to join her in addressing the community. That afternoon, she, Acaraho, Nootau, and Nimida stood at the front of the Great Chamber and waited for the crowd to settle down before beginning.

"Thank you for coming," Acaraho began. "We are meeting again so soon at the request of Nimida, standing here next to me. You are all aware of the attack on Khon'Tor, and she asked me to bring you all together so she could address you."

Nimida found her voice and began. "I want to thank you for the outpouring of support you have given both me and my brother, Nootau. When I found out the truth, I was angry, bewildered, and lost in an onslaught of emotions and reactions that I did not feel equipped to handle. Now, with some time having passed, I am finding my way back to a feeling of normalcy, though life will never be the same as it was because my identity has been re-written by the truth that was recently revealed.

"I am sure many of you are still trying to come to grips with Khon'Tor's confession. And, like you, I am dealing with the disillusionment that even those we look up to the most are fallible. That Leaders can be just as flawed as the rest of us, that they have struggles and challenges just as we do. The truth is, we all fall short. None of us can claim that we have never hurt another person, though I know what Khon'Tor did to my mother is far worse than what most of us could ever inflict. But, I find it uplifting that despite the worst one can do to another, there can still be healing and forgiveness, as Adia has proven to us all.

"I have come, therefore, to ask you please to find forgiveness for Khon'Tor and let the past remain in the past. I believe Adia and Acaraho when they say that none of this was kept a secret for any reason other than to protect our people and this community, which was in a fragile state when it took place. I ask that if you have not already, you find it in your hearts to accept this and not hold it against either Acaraho or Adia that they kept the truth from you. Many of you have known them far longer than I have, and yet I know that they had only our best interests at heart, as in everything they do."

"How are we to forgive Khon'Tor for what he did?" someone called out.

"I am learning that forgiveness is not a straightforward path, and I know from my own experience that there are peaks and valleys along the way. It has not been a matter of deciding at some point in time to forgive him but committing to the process of learning to forgive him. I ask you, please, to search your hearts and find forgiveness so we can all heal together, and whether you find that forgiveness now or later, to pray for his recovery. Think of his innocent mate, Tehya, and their offspring. Remember his years of service as one of the greatest of the People's Leaders. Khon'Tor's life is made up of more than this one dark act. Let humility guide us, and let us lift him up for healing to the One-Who-Is-Three.

"I do not know who attacked Khon'Tor. I hope we do find out someday, as this was a cowardly and condemnable act."

Acaraho then asked Nootau if he wanted to add anything, which he did.

"I agree with everything my sister has just said. We have lived different lives, of course. I grew up here at the High Rocks, raised by two parents in love that any offspring would be blessed to experience. And though learning the truth was a shock to me, it was not as devastating as it no doubt has been for Nimida. So I will add to what she said. If she and my mother can forgive Khon'Tor for his crime, then how can any of us not?

"My sister and I are both paired, and we hope to have offspring someday. I have no idea whether the truth of our parentage is something they will ever need to know or perhaps know only when they are older, and, no doubt, Nimida and I will wrestle with that for some time. But I ask that you please respect our wishes to let us handle this as we see fit. Please do not let gossip be the way they find out about the sins of the past. Allow my sister and me and our mates to parent them as we see best, knowing that we are, ourselves, trying to find our way through everything as best we can.

"Please pray for Khon'Tor to live and to fully recover because revenge is not our way; it has never been. It grieves me terribly that someone within this community took it upon themselves to harm him."

When Nootau had finished, Acaraho thanked everyone for coming, their cue to disperse.

"I hope my words helped," Nimida said

Nootau echoed her sentiment.

"I will be sure to tell Khon'Tor what you both did," Adia said. "I believe it will mean a great deal to him, and the lifting of his spirit can only assist his chances of survival."

CHAPTER 17

Khon'Tor did survive, and eventually, he and his mate were able to return to the Far High Hills under the escort of the most trusted guards of the High Rocks, including First Guard Thetis. Khon'Tor would be under Urilla Wuti's care until he fully healed. Tehya's parents had been taking care of Arismae, Bracht'Tor, and Kweeuu, and the day the couple was reunited with their family was one of the happiest of their lives. But both knew that from then on, their visits to Kthama would be tinged with wariness—that is, if Khon'Tor ever let Tehya go with him again.

Thetis carried a satchel in which were the hood and blade, wrapped in a hide that was securely fastened. Acaraho had decided it would best be kept away from the High Rocks, so Thetis was to deliver the bundle to the Overseer to be kept in a secure place. Perhaps the items would someday provide a clue to the attacker's identity.

The outpouring of support for Adia and Acaraho continued, but as time passed, Adia found herself growing tired of it. She had long ago moved forward and didn't need to revisit that part of her life, though she recognized that it was part of the People's healing process to express their sympathy and support.

She had other worries on her mind because as each day passed, she was drawing closer to the time when Pan would return to claim An'Kru.

One evening on their sleeping mat, safe in her mate's arms, Adia let silent tears flow down her face.

"Please do not cry, Saraste'," Acaraho said as he stroked the mass of her thick dark hair. "I cannot bear to see you unhappy. Tell me how to help you."

"No one can help me, I am afraid. I am so worried about An'Kru's future, and I cannot shake it. In one way, I wish Pan had not told me, but then again, I know she was preparing me so I could make the most of our time together. I am afraid my sadness is also going to affect Aponi and Nelairi, and I do not know where to turn."

"You know I would do anything for you, but I do not know how to help you with this. In the past, you have always turned to the Great Mother, and help has always come."

Adia sniffed and wiped the tears from her face. "You are right, and I have not been praying about this as I should. Perhaps, deep down, I am angry with the

Great Spirit. I thought I had learned long ago that there is no way to prevent troubles from coming and that we have to trust that, with the Great Spirit's help, we will find the strength inside ourselves to handle it. Thank you for reminding me, my love."

Adia wiped the rest of the fresh tears that had just rolled down her cheeks and turned over onto her side, tucking her hands under her cheek.

Acaraho turned and wrapped himself around his mate's form. "I will pray for you too. Now sleep. I am sure you are exhausted on many levels about many things, and perhaps it will look better in the morning."

She nodded, closed her eyes, and tried to quiet her mind.

Adia was not asleep. Instead, she was standing in a grove of towering trees. Far in the background was Kthama's familiar mountain range. It was twilight, and the evening stars were just blinking into view. A warm breeze wafted past, and as it brushed her skin, it felt comforting, like a caress. Everything was more alive, deeper, and richer. She was back in the Corridor.

She looked around, taking in her surroundings. In the past, it had always been daylight, but this time of day was just as beautiful, though it had an even more sacred feel to it. The daytime birds were silent, and in the distance, she could hear the melodious hoot of an owl. A bat wove a lacy path overhead, and only the light whisper of its wings interrupted the silence.

Then, a soft light started to form. It was faint, white with a tinge to it that was almost blue. Adia was mesmerized as she watched it grow slowly bigger and bigger. And as its brightness increased, a deepening sense of deep peace fell over her. It drew her soul as if she were being called to it, but in a manner she could not explain. An undercurrent of joy started to form within her, and the presence she always felt in the Corridor became stronger. Finally, the light became so bright that had she been looking at it with her natural eyes, she would have had to look away.

Adia wondered if it could be E'ranale, though she had not made such an entrance before.

Slowly a figure formed, and she could tell it was a male. A very tall male with a muscular build. The features started to take shape, and within a moment, the most magnificent Akassa she had ever seen stood before her. She knew her mouth was agape, but she couldn't help it.

"Do you not recognize me, Mother?" The voice was deep and resonant, almost melodic—as if the very song of creation was woven through it.

Adia looked the figure up and down. The flowing silver-white hair, the silver-white muscular chest, torso, arms, and legs, their covering more abundant than usual for an Akassa. Meeting her gaze were eyes the color of winter storm clouds that seemed to open into infinity.

"An'Kru? My son?" she managed to gasp out. "I know anything is possible here in the Corridor, yet I am truly—amazed. You have brought me here."

"I could not bear to see you suffer so deeply, so, yes, I brought you here to look upon the son you raised."

Adia wanted to reach out and touch him, but she could not bring herself to.

"Your heart is troubled," he continued. "You are filled with so many worries about how to teach me, how to fill a lifetime of love into a few short years before Pan is to take me away, what the future holds for me. It is more than any mother should have to bear, so I have brought you here to calm your fears."

A million questions tossed about in Adia's mind, like rapids in a raging river, yet she could not form any of them into speech.

"Hear my words and let the truth in them permeate through your soul. My years with you were filled with love and happiness. Every moment of my life, I knew you loved me, I knew you had only my best interests at heart, and I knew I was safe in your care. You taught me with wisdom and kindness, and when the time came for me to leave with Pan, my heart was at peace."

Adia finally found her words. "How could that be? Did you not miss me, miss Kthama?"

"You of everyone can best understand what I am about to say. Just as you were called to be a Healer, so do I have my own life path. The life I live is the life I was born to; this is what I was created for. You could not have found peace in your life on Etera had you denied your life's purpose, and so it is with me.

"Do not cry for me, nor worry about me and where my destiny lies. The dreams you have for me, of the male you want me to grow into, are misplaced. I did not come to live an ordinary life, so let go of your expectations. Accept that I must do what is given to me to do, what is mine alone to do. Let your heart not be troubled; let it rather make peace with this.

"Whether you realize it or not, you have been mourning the life you dreamed of for me. To grow up, to pair, and to have offspring—to live the life any mother would hope for her offspring. But it is my honor, privilege, and joy to serve the Great Spirit with the life given to me to live on Etera. I could only be unhappy if I were to fail; that would grieve me to an extent perhaps no other soul can understand—but I will not fail.

"I love you with all that I am, Mother—and Father, too. Do not grieve over our lost years together. Someday, when your time on Etera is finished, and you begin your journey here, you will experience for yourself how life on Etera is only the blink of an eye. Your final destination is in the eternal arms of the Great Spirit, and one day we will be together for eternity. The joy of that reunion is unimaginable, and the love we shared, and will share, will never leave us."

Adia not only heard her son's words, she felt them, as if they had the ability to pass through her and become part of her being. They buoyed her up, and she felt her entire countenance lifted as peace started to fill her. She could not bear to look away from the deep grey eyes, but she felt herself return to her body, and in the next moment, she felt the warmth and comfort of her mate, still protectively enveloping her.

As it was each time she returned from the Corridor, Adia felt overwhelmed and needed to rest, but she didn't want to sleep. She wanted to relive over and over that visit with her son in the Corridor, to press every detail firmly into her memory. The sights, the sounds, the eternal presence that permeated everything, and the gloriousness of An'Kru. But in no time, she was fast asleep, and she slept more soundly than in all the days since Pan had told her of her son's future.

When Adia awoke the next morning, her heart was far lighter. The fearful anticipation of the future had been lifted, and she felt like herself again. The peace that An'Kru's words had instilled in her remained, and she lay there for a while, basking in it and taking comfort in her mate's deep breathing next to her. First light was just breaking, and as she had not done for a long time, she welcomed the day.

After a few moments, she rose and padded about, putting on her wrap and checking on all three of her offspring. They were still asleep, their forms curled up into precious little balls. She stood watching them, thanking the Great Spirit for An'Kru's healing intervention. She knew now that she could raise them all with no reservations. By giving time to them all, she would make sure that neither Aponi nor Nelairi was disadvantaged by An'Kru's special qualities. She was confident that each would know how much she loved them and that she would delight in discovering who they were in their own rights.

She turned when she heard Acaraho sit up. She watched him stretch, extending his arms overhead. Her gaze traced the line of his muscular arms and shoulders, the broad chest, his handsome face, and she realized then how much her depression must have also affected him. She sat down with him on the sleeping mat. "Shhh. They are all sleeping."

Then she pressed her lips to his and leaned him back on the sleeping mat. His moan of pleasure lifted her heart even further, and she straddled him, caressed his chest, and then reached down and guided him into her. They made love for some time, then rested in each other's arms until the offspring started stirring.

"I have missed you so," Acaraho said as Adia rose to take care of them.

She understood what he meant. "I know, and I will tell you what happened as soon as I finish taking care of the little ones, but the depression and anxiety that have haunted me for so long are gone. I am at peace—with all of it. I know it has also been hard on you, and I thank you for standing with me."

After the offspring were fed and cleaned up, Adia told Acaraho of her visit with An'Kru in the Corridor. He listened silently, his eyes searching her features as she spoke. When she was finished, they prayed together, giving thanks to the Great Spirit for all the blessings in their lives.

As the following days turned into weeks, then months, Adia never lost her sense of wonder when observing An'Kru as he grew and learned. It was hard to reconcile the robust adult male she had met in the Corridor with the toddler before her now. An'Kru's visit had touched her deeply, and its effect had never abated, so she was able to give each of the twins the attention they deserved, undistracted by unrelenting concerns for An'Kru's future.

It was as An'Kru had said; no one could understand better than her what it meant to have a calling and the drive to satisfy it. Only after decades of service as the Healer to the People of the High Rocks did Adia have peace about stepping aside. Only having such a skilled and intuitive Healer as Iella to replace her had quelled all the misgivings she'd had about relinquishing the role. Her desire to help others would never abate, but time had given her the wisdom to see her role more broadly.

Her driving priority now was raising the three

souls who played happily in front of her every day, ensuring that each of them would have as normal an environment as possible and that neither of An'Kru's youngest siblings would feel overshadowed by his uniqueness.

And when it was time for Pan to return and take An'Kru with her, Adia would remember his words—that he was born to this, that it was his destiny, and that he could be no less than it was given to him to be.

As far as anyone knew, the People of the High Rocks kept their promise to the Overseer and Acaraho and did not speak of Khon'Tor's confession outside of their own circles. But the community had been through so much since the time of Khon'Tor's crime and was now so firmly rooted in Acaraho's leadership that the repercussions were far less than they might have been had the truth been revealed when it first happened. Adia had chosen wisely; in sacrificing her own right to justice, she had indeed protected the community she loved. Yes, the People of the High Rocks were rocked by the truth, but the community was not destroyed. The bonds of love and family among the People there were strong enough to endure even this terrible revelation.

Though the attacker had meant to take Khon'-Tor's life in payment for his crime against their

Healer, in a way, the attack had only helped give it back. Nimida and Nootau's impassioned plea to the People to forgive Khon'Tor, coupled with the shock that resulted from the attempt on his life, had helped many of them find their own path to forgiving their former Adik'Tar.

In the Corridor, E'ranale turned to Adia's father, Apenimon'Mok. "A long road still lies ahead for your daughter."

"Yes, and she has already weathered so much," he answered. "E'ranale, Adia believes her son will bring unity to Etera."

"I know," she said, sadly.

AN INTERVIEW WITH THE CHARACTERS

There was quite a gathering waiting to speak with me, so I was a little unsure of what was about to be said!

LR: Well, hello, everyone. How are you feeling now that we are into Series Three?

Khon'Tor: Personally, that was a rough ride. I hope you are not planning anything so difficult for future books. Though, as long as Tehya and our offspring are healthy and safe, that is really all that matters.

Tehya: Do not say that. You matter as much as anyone else, and you are the foundation of my world! But it is distressing that there is someone out there with a desire for revenge against you.

Khon'Tor: If I have any say in it, neither Tehya nor our offspring will be going anywhere near the High Rocks for a long, long time.

LR: I understand, Khon'Tor. Until we know who the attacker is, you have every right to be protective and on guard.

Tehya: So I will not be going with you to the High Rocks again—ever?

Khon'Tor: Your safety will always be my first concern, and you will be safer at the Far High Hills, and I will be safer at the High Rocks without you. If another attack comes, I need to focus on defending myself. I cannot do that and worry about you too.

LR: Does anyone else want to share how they feel now that the first book in Series Three has been written?

Adia: Meeting An'Kru as an adult was totally unexpected, and it did quell my fears about the future. It does not mean I will not be sad when he leaves with Pan or that I will never have other moments of concern. But overall, I am at peace because I understand that for An'Kru not to fulfill his destiny would be worse than any inconvenience or any sorrow that may result.

LR: I am sure he will also miss you, Adia. No one can replace Mama.

Adia: And Nootau will be leaving too. It is good they will have each other, but it is another exercise in letting go and trusting the Great Spirit's wisdom in how it unfolds. I am grateful we will have Iella to take care of while he is gone.

Nimida: I just want to say how grateful I am to Khon'Tor for his confession. It opens the door for me now to actively participate as Adia's daughter and Nootau's sister. I will also greatly miss Nootau when he leaves with Pan and An'Kru, and it will help with that, too. I am sure, by then, I will miss An'Kru as his older sister, but we will all still have the twins.

LR: Acaraho, you are being quiet.

Acaraho: I just have a lot on my mind. What will the future hold for the Brothers? The Waschini threat is only going to escalate, and how will we help them, protect them, since neither my people nor the

Sassen can risk being seen by the Waschini? And from the People's side, we have lived in our communities for thousands of years. Is the white invasion going to drive us from our homes as it is doing with the Brothers? Where would we go?

LR: That is a heavy burden to carry, Acaraho. No one knows what the future holds for your people.

They were all suddenly looking at me strangely.

LR: Okay, well, not *no one;* I know. You don't, but you can, as Adia said, have the faith to trust that you will find the strength to handle whatever it is.

Pan and Moart'Tor stepped in.

Pan: Sorry, we were talking about the story. I have so many questions!

Moart'Tor: So do I, but mostly, I am sad. I know I need to let go of my daydream about Eitel and what we might have shared. I need to be content with my life with Naha. And I need to let my family at Zuenerth find their own path to the truth. I just pray there is one.

Pan: I will do whatever I can to open their eyes, Moart'Tor, I promise you. I just do not yet know how or when the opportunity will arise.

Moart'Tor: I cannot help but think how rich their lives would be—all of them—if they could live here at Lulnomia. But I do understand they have to let go of their hatred for the Akassa and Sassen before they could join the rest of the Mothoc here.

Oh'Dar had not spoken yet. I think he was leaving room for the others to speak first.

Oh'Dar: You are right, Leigh; only you know what is coming for any of us. But I remember you said Acise and I will have more offspring, and I am anxious for that to happen. I know the joy of having a sibling, and I want that for I'Layah. And I can only hope that if we are blessed with more children, they will have time to get to know my grandmother and Ben.

LR: I never knew any of my grandparents, but I know from how others speak of it that having grandparents can be a great blessing.

I looked around at everyone and realized anew how much I have grown to love each of them.

LR: You all look tired.

Tehya: We are. This was an emotional ride for many of us, though the stories usually are.

LR: Book Two is right behind this one, so rest up while you can.

Acaraho: Any chance you will take it easy on us in Book Two?

LR: No promises. I know you have all been through a lot, but try to remember that no matter how bad it looks, things have always worked out in the end.

Each indicated agreement in their own way, and one by one, eventually left me. So, now, on to Book Two!

PLEASE READ

I can only assume that since you have read the first book in Series Three, you have already read those in Series One and Two, so I thank you for your loyalty and interest in my stories.

If you have not already left a rating or review for each of the books in these series, I humbly ask if you would go and do so now. You can find the link to *Write a Product Review* through your Amazon account. If you bought a digital copy, it will be under *Orders / Digital Orders*. If you bought a paperback copy, it will be under *Your Orders*.

I know this is asking a lot, as there are now nineteen books, but it lets other potential readers know that those who have read them truly found them worthwhile.

You can simply leave a star rating if you do not wish to make a comment. Of course, 5 stars is the best an author can hope for.

Reviews on Goodreads are also greatly appreciated. The site address is:

https://www.goodreads.com/author/show/19613286.Leigh_Roberts

Series Three will continue for several books. You can join my newsletter to get updates at the link below:

https://www.subscribepage.com/theeterachroniclessubscribe

Or you can follow my author page on Amazon:

https://www.amazon.com/Leigh-Roberts/e/B07YLWG6YT

You can email me at:

contact@leighrobertsauthor.com

If you have not yet done so, you can join the private Etera Chronicles Facebook group!

https://www.facebook.com/groups/398774871015260

However you decide to join me, I do hope you will. I love hearing from you, and your feedback and comments are very valuable to me.

Thank you! See you in Book Two of Series Three!

Blessings - Leigh

ACKNOWLEDGMENTS

Here we are together, at the dawn of Series Three. It has been a long journey but a satisfying one. When I set out to write, I had no idea how important my support system would be. Long hours jotting down ideas, culling them, adding more. Rushing to find a notepad when inspiration hit at peculiar times. But I would soon learn that two of the most important people in this process are my husband and my editor. Without their support, I would not have published any of these books, let alone be going into Series Three.

To my husband, Greg, who has stood by me the entire journey, sacrificing our personal time together so I could sit at the computer and type for hours on end, thank you for your complete support.

To my editor, Joy, who, along the way, has become a trusted and dear friend. I depend on her to make the writing the best it can be, to bounce ideas off of, and to keep me straight when I get something wrong. Which happens more than you might think despite my charts, tables, and spreadsheets!

They say if you have two people to stand by you, you are blessed. And so, I am blessed indeed.

Made in the USA
Las Vegas, NV
20 February 2024